Edwin Arnold

Adzuma or the Japanese Wife

A Play in Four Acts

Edwin Arnold

Adzuma or the Japanese Wife
A Play in Four Acts

ISBN/EAN: 9783337165499

Printed in Europe, USA, Canada, Australia, Japan

Cover: Foto ©Andreas Hilbeck / pixelio.de

More available books at **www.hansebooks.com**

ADZUMA

OR

The Japanese Wife

A PLAY IN FOUR ACTS

BY

SIR EDWIN ARNOLD

AUTHOR OF " THE LIGHT OF ASIA," "JAPONICA," ETC., ETC.

NEW YORK

CHARLES SCRIBNER'S SONS

1893

DRAMATIS PERSONÆ

MORITO MUSHA ENDO .   a Japanese Nobleman.

KAMEJU   .   .   .   his faithful Retainer.

SAKAMUNE   .   .   .   his companion, a Samurai.

WATARU WATANABE   .   { another Japanese Nobleman, husband of Adzuma.

SASAKI .   .   .   .   Lord of Idzu.

HOJO TOKIMASA .   .   a Samurai.

DOI MORINAGA   .   .   the same.

ADACHI SANEHIRA   .   the same.

A FISHERMAN.

A LAMPSELLER.

ADZUMA   .   .   .   { Wife of Wataru, and daughter of Koromogawa.

KOROMOGAWA   .   .   Mother of Adzuma.

O YOSHI }
O TAMA }   .   .   .   Waiting-ladies.

Retainers, Soldiers, Attendants, Citizens, Priests, Musumes, Robbers, &c.

PROLOGUE

Lest aught offend you, in our foreign Play,

Let me—for him that writ it—briefly say,

'Tis a true story of the old Japan,

Where they who will the changeless strife may scan

Of fateful mortal passions; and, beside,

See in our Adzuma, high-typified,

The gentle, patient, faithful Nippon wife

Done to the fashion of the faultless life

Which those did learn to lead, by ancient rules

And manners shut away from Western schools.

Here shall be seen, too, how the doctrine grew

That past, forgotten, years constrain the new,

And souls are born, with life-scores incomplete

Which start anew when seeming strangers meet.

But, most and best of all, here shall you see

How "dear to Heaven is saintly Chastity,"

And Death himself but friend and minister

To Adzuma, and noble hearts like her.

ADZUMA,

OR

THE JAPANESE WIFE.

ACT I.

SCENE 1.—KYÔTÔ.

An outer Guard-Room of the Emperor's Palace. Armed Samurai and Soldiers standing or sitting about.

HOJO. Saw you young Lord Morito throw Sakamune in the wrestling-ring to-day?

ADACHI. Aye! a notable shoulder-heave it was! Sakamune, for all his skill, rolled over the edge of the platform like a pine-log down the bank of Katsura.

HOJO. *Naruhodo!* What a man that is! Every inch of him soldierly!

Doi. He is now in high favour. When came he first to the Court?

Hojo. It was just after Morito won back the Emperor's favourite horse, Tama-jishi, which had been so boldly stolen by the robber Koroku, whom none of us could come at.

Doi. Did he do that?

Hojo. Yes! he was only a stripling, but he could swim the sea like a *tai;* and run so fleetly that a cord of thirty *shaku*, tied to his waist, would stream in a straight line behind him. With Kameju, his retainer, who is as prudent as Morito is headstrong, he went to Tosa in Tango, where the outlaw made his hold.

Doi. What could they look to do against Koroku?

Hojo. That which courage does, backed by wit. They gave themselves out as pilgrims to the thirty-three shrines, weary and in need: two wandering youths, one tall and stout, the other delicate as a musume, but both of the presence to please Koroku. So he entertained them well, and, on a time, questioned them if they knew the military arts, wanting them for his band.

Doi. How answered they?

Hojo. Kameju answered, saying, it was to their shame that, albeit sons of a Daimio, a peasant had brought them up, and taught them only to swim, ride, and wrestle. So the Robber would see them show their skill. Kameju plunged into the waves, and swam well, but Morito, taking a knife in his belt, dived from the rocks and brought up, dead, a large *fuka*, of a bow's length. Then they were put to wrestle, in which Morito, designing that Kameju should win, and thus be first chosen to ride the great horse, gave his companion advantage, and was finally thrown; yet not until they had played before Koroku like young tigers. So Kameju was to mount the horse first, to show who could ride best; and well he handled the black stallion, which none of the thieves dared bestride. But hardly was he mounted, and beginning speed, before Morito, quicker than any deer on Arashiyama, darts after him, and while all the rogues thought it the wantonness of the youth, he leaps up behind Kameju, claps heel to the stallion's flank, and ere the robbers could so much as get to saddle, they had seen the last of the Emperor's horse.

DOI. For this he was taken to favour?

HOJO. It is so. And ever since he has constantly bettered his fortunes by deeds of service. Yet there is a wild spirit under his knightliness which only Kameju can restrain.

ADACHI. *Domo!* did we not see to-day, when Saka-mune took him in the "bear's grip," how young Morito's teeth clenched; how he breathed; how he braced; how he set his feet like stone gate-posts, and flung forth his very good friend with a wrench that would have sent a *koku* of rice flying?

HOJO. *Nē?* But, afterwards he raised Sakamune full courteously, and wiped the dust out of his mouth with his own head-cloth.

ADACHI. It was so! it was so! nevertheless Morito's

glance, in that clinch, was like an eagle's look when it draws the curtain off its eyes.

Doi. You are honourably right! Meseemed Sir Sakamune did not show best pleased to be grounded so rudely before the ladies of the Court.

Hojo. Ah, you marked that? I, too, thought he scowled more than a beaten player should, when he rose; albeit he is a very polished Knight, who lets none see what is hid in the silk sleeve of his manners. But you, Adachi! went your speech, just now, deeper than its words, when you likened Morito's look to an eagle's?

ADACHI. Nay, Sir! I spoke only as I have seen.

Hojo. 'Tis the more strange, because there is told a tale by the priests and the women—a story of *shura* and of *hoben**—giving out that in a former existence our Morito was indeed an eagle.

ADACHI. *Naruhodo;* honourably make us hear.

Hojo. In truth, I am but partly versed in the

---

* *Shura* is " blood-feud "—*hoben* is " divine decree :" both Buddhist terms.

matter, but here comes one who can tell us all, if he
will speak. Ask Kameju Haruki, the Heimin, if you
would know.

Enter KAMEJU.

KAMEJU. " The day," fair gentlemen !

HOJO.   To you " the day ! "
   What news, Kameju ?

KAM.   Only soldiers' news ;
   Morito takes your watch at hour of the Ox.

DOI. His name was large this moment on our tongues.

KAM. They could not wag, sirs ! to a nobler one ;
   Morito Musha Endo, my good Lord,
   Can give you talk enough from sun to sun
   If what you love to talk upon be deeds
   Fitting a warrior, and his Father's son.

HOJO. We know your mind to him, and his deserts,
   And none is minded save to praise him here,
   But, when you cast your *zori* at the gate,
   Our speech went on the story of his birth ;
   An eagle mixed with it, and foregone feuds,

So was it said—and you the one who knows :

An't be not private, will you make it ours ?

KAM. Sirs ! what the priests talk at the evening rice

And women in the bath-house, may well come

To all your ears, if soldiers' ears can care

For matter vague and visionary as mist

Driving down Biwa; which the East wind blows

To shapes of dragon, devil, bird, and snake,

Melting before you name them.

ADACHI.   Still, 'tis known

Our past lives build the present, which must mould

The lives to be.

KAM.   Oh, if you hold to that,

I had as lief my honoured Lord drew birth

From eyries, as from any plainer nests.

What ? must you have it ?

HOJO.   Deign augustly, Sir !

KAM. Then, since 'tis chatter with us, this they say—

The gossips at the wells—Two reigns ago,

The Emperor Toba ruling, a vast Bird

Haunted Shiki-no-kami's craggy crest,

In Yamato ; a monstrous snow-white Bird,

Its spread wings like the mid-sails of a junk,

Its beak a blacksmith's shears, its talons twinned

Hooks of grey bronze.   And, when the women laid

Their babes upon the rice sheaves, oftentimes

A whistle would be heard amidst the pines

As if a typhoon burst, and there would pass

The roar of those wide, terrible, white vans

Casting a quick-gone shadow, and be heard

The scream of the eagle, swooping on the babe

With orbs ablaze, and silencing the wail—

Save for the mother's ears—of that soft prey

Whose tender limbs the savage talons gripped

And bore aloft ; while some ran for their bows,

And some flung foolish stones, and some made
     speed

To follow, if they might, the Ravisher ;

Yet always, to the hollows of his hill

Safe he took flight.

Doi.   They speak in Yamato

Now, of that plague.

Kam.   Well, then, the Emperor heard,

And vowed the plague should stay.   Therefore

he chose

Lord Yasuhira from his list of lords,

Best at the archery ; bade him fare forth

And slay the eagle.   Now this knight was old ;

His wife, Koromogawa, childless still,

And near past nursing-times.   So both went up

To Kwannon's temple at the lotus-pool

Praying these two boons—that a child might come

To take the enlarging honours of their name,

And that some happy arrow from his string

Might find the fierce Bird's breast, and save the

folk.

Thus, day by day, and night by night, alone—

With Yasuhira gone—his lady prayed

These things unceasingly at Kwannon's shrine

Till answer came—strange answer, were all true !

ADACHI. The Gods do listen, if we ask enough.

KAM. I know not; but they say it did befall

That,—one day, in her garden, plucking flowers

To set before the goddess—from the reeds

Koromogawa sees a bright snake creep

Which, with soft rustlings, seeks to come to her.

No loathsome reptile, but a lovely coil

Of gold and green—if one can like a snake—

All living, jewelled silk.   Thereon, the maids

Cried out and ran ; but Yasuhira's wife

Was none afeard, and stroked the glistering
    length

Of the cold worm, and let its black forked tongue

Play with her hand ; then, put it gently back,

Straightway forgetting.

DOI.   For the life of me

I could not play with serpents.

KAM.   Well, that night,

Lying a-bed, she heard a beat on the screen

A whisper, " Open ! open ! "   Whereupon,

All Knight's wife as she was, she snatched a spear

And slid the *shoji* back, and look ! a form

Oh, passing, peerless, fair ; a lovely face

Delicate-featured, as of some young maid

Budding to woman, but the garb a man's,

Dark blue *hakama*, swinging purple sleeves,

The long, smooth, gleaming hair tied like a man's,

Girdle of 'broidered silk, and from its folds   -

Two sword-hilts forking.   If there dwelt a Dame

Leal to her Lord, 'twas Yasuhira's wife ;

Yet, while she eyed him, in herself she said,

" Thou gracious one ! if thou be'est man indeed

For thee Komachi's snow-cold blood had thaw'd,

For thee the Princess Chiyo's breast of stone

Had turned to flame ! Oh, that thou wert my child ! "

HOJO. Komachi and the other were of those

Whom no man's love could touch ?

KAM.   So 'tis ; and when

She put the *shoji* back, saying : " Who comes

By night-time o'er the fence, is no true man

But *kusemono,* but a plunderer ! ''

A gentle voice wailed : '' Yasuhira's wife !

Give entrance ! think thou not ill thoughts of me

That am thy lover, past all words of love,

And cannot choose but be about thy steps

By day-time, 'mid the flowers ; and in the night,

Where thou dost sleep.'' '' Begone ! '' the Lady
    cries :

'' My Lord is absent, and I see no man

By day or night ! I know thee not, begone !

Or I must strike thee with my husband's spear ! ''

'' Nay ! but thou knowest me,'' the soft voice says :

'' In many shapes I have been nigh to thee,

Because I yearn, out of the shadowy world

To come to earth by thee, and be thy child ;

And this noon, in the garden, that was I

Who crept, a snake, out from the water-weeds

And would have fondled longer those dear hands

But that, unkind, thou dravest me away

With thy bunched lilies.''

ADACHI.   *Naruhodo !* Sir,

  To hear a snake talk so !

KAM.   For very shame

  To hear a snake enamoured of her so

  Again she lifts the spear : but the form said :

  " Strike ! if thou wilt, since, in another life,

  I shall be woman, and more near to thee

  As I am now thy servant and thy friend

  Whose life is thine, to live and die for thee."

  On this spake Koromogawa : " If 'tis sooth,

  Go where my husband is, and help him kill

  The great white eagle haunting Yamato."

  Answered the beauteous shape : " Straight will I
     speed,

  For this is easy, and my destiny

  To give myself for thee, whom I shall meet

  In other lives, and other—till the end."

DOI. Judge you, good Sir ! 'twas waking truth, or
     dream ?

KAM. She would have held it for a dream, but, see !

At day-dawn, on the cover of her bed

Lies a long snake - slough — gold and green and
    blue

And purple, like the apparel of the Form :

And, afterwards, what did befall, seems more.

ADACHI. Ah ! *Nama Amida !* we long to hear.

KAM. Her lord comes back with pomp and beating
    drums,

Four men bearing the vast bird on a pole,

Its white plumes bloodied. And his speech was this

When, full of honours from the Emperor,

He sate at home again. " I fared, my wife,

To Yamato, and prayed the Goddess long

For those two boons, the first a boy or girl

To bear th' enlarging honours of our house,

And next that I might find and slay the Bird.

Far did I wander over hill and moor

With notch on string, searching the speckless
    sky,

Threading black pine-woods, rousing spotted deer

From glens unvisited, and startling up

The wild crane from her eggs, the grunting boar

Foul from his lair, and solitary bears

From berry-thickets where no man had come ;

Yet nothing nearer won I to my quest :

Till, on the seventh day, ranging at dawn

I spy a sugi-tree, whose swaying top,

A hundred arrow-lengths in air, spread there

Like a green cloud ; and, in its topmost fork

The piled sticks of an eagle's eyrie, loud

With clamours of the hungry couplets.   See !—

While I get breath and hide—a noise in the blue,

A whir of strong-struck pinions, and there lights,

Shaking the mighty tree, that great white Bird,

Its claws drove deep in the dead velvet meat

Of some poor mother's nursing babe.

                          How reach

At such a height the tyrant ?   Pondering this

I mark a bright snake, from beneath the nest,

Glide near and nearer till it flings its coils—

Quick as a sword-blade springing—round the Bird

Chaining his strong wings down, fettering his feet,

Binding him tight with fold on glistening fold ;

And—while he screams and tumbles on his tree—

Darting on this and that side of his throat

The venomed daggers of its wide red jaw,

Which struck, and, once more struck.   Thereat,
the Bird

Cries loud for rage, and in its crooked beak

Mashes the Serpent's head ; but sick and bound,

Falls to a lower fork, locked with his foe ;

And there a shaft can reach him.   To my ear

I drew my string, and loosed ; the bow sang loud,

The arrow flew, the keen steel pierced and pinned

Serpent and Bird in one close writhing mass

Which bounded, plume and scale, from bough to
bough

And rolled down, dead and reddened, at my
foot."

HOJO. *Ma !* Kameju ! no better tale-teller

Holds the still people on the *Yose*-mats!

And how fits this with Endo Morito?

KAM. Since you hold patience yet, that shall be told.

Lord Yasuhira finished, saying thus,

With solemn face: " Once more in Yamato

I sought the shrine, and gave the goddess thanks,

And slept; but, sleeping saw One not of our
world,

Radiant and great, who spake: ' Seen lives of men

Intermix close with other lives unseen.

What is done well, obedient to the Law,

Blossoms in bliss, and what is wrongly done

Withers to woe, 'till it be purged. Thy prayers

Were heard! The snake that helped thee must
be born

A beauteous daughter to thy wife. The Bird

Hath ended all save one hard penitence

For which once more he meets the Snake, and
. strives.

He will be Morimitsu's son on earth,

2

Born of Shiraito.   Lest thy waking sense

This vision scorn, a sign is given for faith.'

And, when the morning-cock crowed me awake

In my hand, wife ! there lay an eagle's plume,

With a snake's scale.''

HOJO.   Partly I knew all this before, but never
nearly so well, as to-day.   Our thanks, good Kameju !
That's why Koromogawa, then, Adzuma's mother,
would liever have fire take her house, than Morito
Endo and her daughter come together.

KAM.   I have prated too much, already ; but, indeed,
I deem the fortune of my Lord lies better elsewhere.
These things are as they must be.   We talk like
waiting-maids in a tea-house ; and 'tis time, I think,
that the guard was shifted.

END OF SCENE I.

ACT I.

SCENE 2.

A Garden of the Palace, laid out in the Japanese style, with rocks, dwarf-trees, bridges, fish-ponds, stone lanterns, etc., etc.

Enter SAKAMUNE.

SAKAMUNE. I would I could dare more, or did hate less !

Three in this world make the world ill to me,

But when I seek how to be quits with them

The fearful half in me pulls at the sleeve

Of the bolder half, and bids me take good heed

Lest when I dig them pits I fall therein.

First of the three, Wataru most I hate—

My friend, a goodly man—because he sleeps

Nightly in that sweet paradise I sought,

Adzuma's arms ; her thrice, thrice happy Lord !

And next I hate, as hot as once I loved,

Adzuma's self, who had no eyes for me

When I did ask her for my wife—and there

Her mother shares my spite, Morito's Aunt.

Last comes Lord Morito—also my friend,

Also most goodly ! oh, a soldier forged

Of stuff as fine as any Bizen blade ;

Yet doth he cross me, and doth humble me,

Holding the manly mirror of his force

Up to this face of weakness I would hide.

A headstrong lord withal, whom I can bring

With craft to the slaughter, as a butcher leads

His brute ox by the nose-ring.   Craft shall do't.

I will devise that each one pushes each

To tears and ruin, while I laugh and watch,

Always '' Kind Sakamune ! honest friend ! ''

But were I otherwise, if that in me

Which should be soldier, matched my pitiless
    mind—

This way were pleasanter, and short to take :

    [*He draws one of his two swords, and lops off the
        top of a young pine-tree.*]

Wataru's head rolled in the dust—like that !

[*He cuts off another pine-tree top.*]

Morito's proud brows rolling—like to that !

[*He aims to cut off a stalk of flowering Golden Lily, but pauses in the blow.*]

And Adzuma's—!   But, oh thou Lily-Flower,

That art so fair, so pure, scented so sweet

As if the Angels' breaths came with thee here ;

And dropped with purple gouts, and rosy stains,

And dusted with pale gold, all like the moles,

And birth-marks, and the ambered silken glow

Of Adzuma, to show fairness more fair,

The white skin whiter, and to draw the eye

Into the madness of the wondering mind,

The longing hand, the yearning hungry blood !

Thus would I end thee, and my aches for thee

Not by some too kind stroke, but so !—and so !

[*He plucks and breaks slowly to pieces a Lily-blossom.*]

Crushing thy sweet, desired, unwilling heart—

The rose, gold, purple, white—all, to one wrack

Of scattered satin leaf, and silver stem,

And soft green cup! Oh, thus! thus! thus! and thus!

That if I wear them not, none other shall,

And that thy soul exhale, in dew of tears,

Sweet incense to the nostrils of my wrong.

Enter MORITO ENDO.

MORITO. Why, Sakamune! do you practise sword-play with the trees and flowers?

SAKAMUNE. Ah! Morito; truly you have caught me idling! I was meditating I know not what. 'Tis a new blade the sword-maker Masamura hath forged for me, and, having it in hand, I tried a cut or two.

MOR. 'T would be better training if the Emperor's saplings and lilies borrowed the bees' stings, and went armed! Steel upon steel is what teaches a soldier, and it has been said well:—"The girded sword is the living soul of the Samurai." Grant me a respectful glance at your new *katana*.

SAKA. It is at your honourable service, like him that owns it.

MOR. My ever good friend! In truth, an excellent piece of sword-craft! the *mune* solid, yet not over-weighted; the *hira* delicate, but firmly-fashioned; and the *nioi* marks playful as watered silk, yet misty as the breath of a musume upon her looking-glass. You must stain such an edge in our next wars with better blood than pine-juice!

SAKA. I hope it may be at your side, then, to show me how swords should be wielded.

MOR. *Domo!* What have I ever done? You are too kind to me. I sought you here, in truth, to ask your forgiveness about the wrestling-match this morning. I fear I handled you rudely.

SAKA. It was my fit punishment for challenging a better man.

MOR. Nay, thou art my master in the ring, and it was only by a false step that I flung thee. But indeed, there is that in my elements, which a friend

must find grace to put by. I desire to live knightly—
but, at times, there comes upon me a passion which
has no conscience. When I felt that thou wouldst
trip me, the evil spirit arose. I am quiet as a pigeon
with a full crop until it rouses, and then 'tis as 'twere
an eagle's wrath, which sets my breast on fire, and
brings the lightning to my eyes. Give me thy forgiveness !

SAKA. It is nothing, it is nothing !

MOR. No ! but 'twas less than friendly that I should
take thee so, when thy leg slipped on the sweat of
my thigh. I am very humbly sorry, and I have
said it elsewhere, that thou art my teacher in the
wrestling-ring.

SAKA. I say it was nothing.

MOR. Then you will bear no grudge ? That is
gracious ! I had a little thing further to declare.
The great new bridge in the City square is to be
opened to-morrow, and I am appointed to keep the
way with five *shotai* of soldiers, and to receive the

Emperor's procession. Also I was to choose my second in the commandment, and I have named thy name, Sakamune !

SAKA. Now thou dost right courteously raise up a fallen foe. I thank thee, Morito Endo! At what hour do we gather ?

MOR. At the hour of the Rat.

SAKA. And where post we our fellows?

MOR. On the south end of the bridge, where the open place is. If the Emperor be well pleased with the doings of the day, there will be another fief for thee ; or, mayhap, a sword of honour wherewith to chop lilies and fir-tops, until better business comes. Sayonara !

SAKA. Sayonara ! and my best service.

> [*Exit* MORITO.
>
> Aye ! proud Bird,
>
> That hast, indeed, the old life rank in thee,
>
> So com'st thou to my springe, full-winged ! This
>
> hap

Brings what I sought. Now shall they blindly
>meet,

Morito and the lovely, spotless wife

Who dwells as high o'er my desire—and his—

As yonder evening star above this pool

Where the frogs croak. Beyond my love thou art,

Adzuma, with the honeyed mouth, but not

Beyond my hate ! Ah, far star ! thou shalt know

Better shine lowly than have me for foe !

[*Exit,* SAKAMUNE.

END OF SCENE 2.

ACT I.

SCENE 3.

An apartment in the house of WATARU WATANABE. *His wife, the* LADY ADZUMA, *and her mother* KOROMOGA-WA, *are discovered, sitting upon the mats, and convers-ing. A samisen (Japanese guitar) lies near at hand.*

KOROMOGAWA. At what time will thy Lord make the august return.

ADZUMA. I know not surely, Mother, but at his first freedom. Ah, I am a too happy woman to say so much, but here only, and only with me, finds he delight. What have I done to be the luckiest wife in all Japan? Hither will he hasten as soon as the Palace duty can be laid aside; and my life will begin anew, as the sea-flower on the rock re-opens when the tide comes back to it.

KOROMO. The Kami-sama grant thee long years of such innocent content! And, indeed, he is a good

Lord, and gentle, and gallant. But it is dangerous
to be overfond for us women, who must abide, and
obey, and rest patient under all things.

ADZUMA. Ah ! teach me how to love a little, then ;

But, in the learning, like a scholar stayed

At the first hard word, I should shut my book,

And blot with tears the new unlovely love,

And change my page ; and so begin again

The old, sweet, easy lesson,—needing not

Teacher, nor school—to love him every day

A little more than yesterday, if that

Doth not do wrong to yesterday's great love

Which filled my heart so full, there seemed no
   room

For any richer morrows. Is there fear

A wife may overgive herself, to pay

In duty, dearness, pleasure, service, smiles,

Her debt of loving to her wedded Lord

Who loves her, keeps, and guards and cherishes ?

Oh ! that might haply be where men will mete

So much, and so much—like commodities—

Of trust, and truth, and faith, and tenderness,

And dole each portion forth ; " this for thy kiss ;

And this to hold thee patient, if I see

Some fairer face outside ; and this because

Thou hast my name, art mother to my child,

And holdest watch upon the money-bags."

Even then 'twere fit, I think—as good wives use

Here in Japan—we did not count with him

Koban for *Koban* of heart's golden coin,

But gave him all, in fast obedience,

And dutifulness, and delight to serve ;

Attending 'till his man's heart trimmed th' account

And paid late interest for fidelities.

But for me, Mother, and this most dear Lord

Who lays, with both great generous palms, palm-
full,

His honour, and his name, and love, and life,

And hours, and days, and joys, and thoughts, and
heart

In these small, feeble, idle hands of mine,

How should I love him with a lesser love

Than all the utmost of my grateful soul,

And my glad body, and my faithful blood ?

Part paying, as the bankrupt traders do,

With all my estate the debt too great to reach,

And then a joyous prisoner in the gaol

Of still unsatisfied expectancy ?

KOROMO. My gentle Adzuma!   I praise your words.

ADZUMA. Mother ! do you remember how we met—

What strange beginnings of this joy to be ?

KOROMO. Well do I call it to mind, Daughter.   You grew up too fair for my peace ; and many a suitor begged you of me.   Sakamune the Samurai, you know, was one ; and the Lord of Idsu ; and Kameju's father, the good Dôsen, also besought me to bestow you upon Morito ; yet I would not.

ADZ. How I do thank you, now, Mother !

KOROMO. Oh, I had deep reasons !   There are destinies which must not mingle ; and besides you took it all out of my hands, Adzuma-chan! falling in love with Wataru.

ADZ. Yes, yes! he was the one man in the world, and the Goddess herself gave him to me.

KOROMO. I think, indeed, he was the gift of our Lady of Mercy. Together we went to the temple of Hase, where I prayed hard that she would choose a good husband for you. Oh, how often I pulled the *tsuna*, and struck upon the *dora!* For six days I prayed, and there seemed no answer coming. On the seventh we met Wataru, riding with Sakamune.

ADZ. Yes, under the white cherry-trees.

KOROMO. Oh, you remember well enough, Adzuma-chan. And how shy you were! But I, who saw your eyes meet, knew Kwannon Sama had sent me my son-in-law.

ADZ. *Okkâsan!* how beautiful and noble he looked! And that evening again I saw him from the balcony of our Inn.

KOROMO. He saw you too, little fox! but you did

not then guess what words of love he had sent to me about you. Yet was I perplexed, for fair fruit may cover evil seeds, and I could not know whether he was surely Kwannon's grace to us, or only a handsome Knight that chanced. *Naruhodo*, then the dreams came !

ADZ. Aye, Mother, how strange and sweet they were ! Oft-times has Wataru told me since, so that I am certain we had the same vision. It seemed to him that, awake and wandering with love-thoughts of me, he came to our Inn, ascended the stair-way, and, although there were fifty chambers, found mine at once, and pushed back a little the *shoji* of it. Then saw he me musing by the lamp-light, you and the serving-girls lying asleep. And, being true Knight, he would not, of course, enter unbidden— but I rose, and beholding again that dear and noble countenance, put softly back the door, and drew him within.

KOROMO. That was too bold, my Child !

ADZ. Ah! Mother, it was in a dream, remember!

KOROMO. Well, and what spake he?

ADZ. Words so tender that I could only tell them to you.

KOROMO. Tell me!

ADZ. He said:

" Dear Lady! from the Mansion of the Moon—
Whose face is moonlight, and whose loosened locks
Frame its fair glory in with clouds of night—
Take not again to Heaven those heavenly eyes,
Those brows as delicate as distant hills
By evening misted, those red-tinctured lips
Which are like new-blown cherry-blossoms, moist
With morning-dew. I do not know your name,
Nor why I love you so, nor what deep spell
Brings me, too daring, to your folded feet;
But I know this, that now for life and death,
Thine am I, and thine only, heart and soul,
I, Watanabe! "

KOROMO. What spake you?

3

ADZ.   I said :

" *Warawa ga na Adzuma*—Sweet Sir ! "—

Thus I made answer in that happy dream,

" My name unfamed is Adzuma, my sire

Was Yasuhira.   We were hither come

To pray the Goddess.   And, because mine heart

Went to you with my eyes when we did meet,

I wish no other man in all this earth

To be my Lord ;   and, if you love me so,

I now will love you, yes, for life and death·

Chiyo mo kawaranu fufu zo."

Oh, I could talk so bold only in dreams !

KOROMO. And afterwards ?

ADZ. Why, then the morning light shot through
the *mado*, and I arose, and gave him for a love-gift,
—always in the vision,—my *koro*, the silver incense-
pot I ever used ; and he gave to me one of the bodkins
from his short sword.

KOROMO. All this in the dream ?

ADZ. Yes ! but it was so true a dream that when

day came we had each beheld the very same vision; and in his hand at his Inn lay my silver incense-cup, while in mine, as thou thyself did'st see, dear Mother, was the bodkin missing from his sword.

KOROMO. It was so, daughter, and I did not doubt thereafter that the Daibosatsu himself, the Great Compassionate One, had given Wataru to you. Sing me now a little song, Adzuma - chan! I love the *samisen.*

ADZ. If it be your honourable pleasure. What shall I sing?

KOROMO. Whatever you will.

ADZ. Then this one, "*Haori kakushite,*" since my Lord likes it well.

[*She sings, accompanying herself upon the samisen.*]

> *She hid his cloak,*
> *She plucked his sleeve,*
> *"To-day you cannot go!*
> *To-day, at least, you must not leave*
> *The heart that loves you so!"*
> *The window she undid*

And back the shutters slid ;
　　And clinging, cried : " Sweet Lord ! perceive
The whole white world is snow ! "
　　　　[A noise of door-opening is heard without.]

ADZ. *Oya ! oya !* It is his voice, his footstep ! I must go to welcome him home.

　　[The house-servants call out " O kaeri ! o kaeri ! "
　　　　and open the shoji.]

Enters WATURU ; ADZUMA *kneels to him on the threshold, saluting.*

O kaeri irrashai ! Vouchsafe august return ! well art thou welcome, dear Lord !

WATARU. *Arigato !* Again I hang in your sweet eyes ! Is all well ?

ADZ. Now thou art here, all is well ! Be honourably pleased to sit ! Did you think, this long while, upon Adzuma ?

WAT. Can a man think without a heart ?

ADZ. Nay, surely ! there would be no thought or life if the bosom's beat were lacking.

WAT. Then, truly, I thought not even once upon thee, pretty one! for my heart was left here behind me, in your lap.

ADZ. Ah! let me keep it there still. I will take such care of it!

WAT. The august Mother! *Ohayo!* [*He salutes* KOROMOGAWA, *with his forehead on the mats.*] Is the honourable health good!

KOROMO. I thank you lovingly. It is good.

WAT. What! have you been at the music?

KOROMO. *Domo!* You know Adzuma cannot live without singing and poetry. And I, also, love the music well. What have you brought with you in these cloths?

WAT. 'Tis a trifle of biwa-fruit and sweet cakes from the Emperor's kitchen for you, *haha-sama!* And for Adzuma some broidered silk for a girdle, and a lacquered writing-box for her poetry-making.

ADZ. Ah, then! thou didst indeed think upon me, false one! But now come to thine ease, and let

me be thy squire, and untie thine armour and thy
sword-belt.

> [*She unfastens and removes* WATARU'S *swords and
> military dress, and adjusts upon him the loose
> Yukata, the " house-gown," and soft silken
> belt, sanjaku-obi.*]

KOROMO. Give me leave, Wataru san ! I will bid
the maids prepare *gozen* for thee. Wilt thou have
roasted eels to-night, or shall they boil thee a fat
koi from the fish-pond ?

WAT. As it falls, good Mother ! as it falls ! 'Tis
meat and drink enough for me to lay aside my iron,
and to sit safe again in my own house.

> [*Exit* KOROMOGAWA.

Close, close, kind wife ! Ah, from the noisy main,
Where roll and break rough waves of salt affairs,
Ambitions, plans, policies, plots and wars,
And the wild winds blow of our mortal weather,
How good it is to be the ship that shoves
Straight o'er the furrowed sea, with sails braced
    square

And helm set hard for port ; and, so to come—

The holiday breezes whistling in the ropes,

The merry dolphins racing us for sport,

The friendly headlands shutting safely in,

The billows gently falling from their foam

To peace, and equal ripples—into port,

And there cast anchor, where the quiet keel

Rides doubled on her shadow in the Sun.

ADZ. Yea, and dear ship ! how good to be the port

Which, glad to have her noble vessel home,

Opens its heart to take the brave bulk in !

Forget upon my breast what storms did swell,

What evil weathers irked, what troublesome seas

Dashed at thy gallant bows their bitter spray,

Or sought to snatch thine ensign, where it flew

Bright emblem of thy bold nobility.

Here art thou safe, indeed, for 'twixt the brunt

Of any outer tempest brewed for thee,

Or distant gathering of dark clouds that brood

Woe to the seaman, stand my steadfast guards,

My harbouring arms, my love, humble but strong,

My life wrapped round thine honour and thy life

Even like the haven-walls, that must go down

Before the ship within takes injury.

WAT. Dear placid Port ! I moor, and rest in thee.

Enter O TAMA.

TAMA. Sir Sakamune stands at the gate, and would
have admission. It is an urgent business.

WAT. Why then, give him honourable entrance ! 'Tis
a well-spoken knight.

Enter SAKAMUNE.

SAKAMUNE. Salutations to this august House ! The
Lady Adzuma ! In truth 'tis long since I hung in those
most honourable eyes !

Enter KOROMOGAWA.

Oh ! and the Lady Koromogawa ! *Makoto ni shibu-
raku !* Is the high health well ?

WAT. We thank you, well !

SAKA. I make unexcused intrusion. Pray you, for-give! but, indeed, I am come upon a well-meant er-rand.

WAT. In any case, you are welcome, Sir Samurai! Condescend to take this cushion.

SAKA. I humbly thank you. And I thank the beau-tiful Lady of the house, and the august Mother.

WAT. You will touch a cup of saké with us, fair Sir?

SAKA. I beseech your lofty pardon! I come but to go. My horse outside draws quick breath from the speed which brought me hither.

KOROMO. What made you ride so hard?

SAKA. To-morrow, Madam! the Emperor opens, in all state, our new bridge in Kyôtô. It will be a gallant sight! I am second in charge of the show, and have at command fine places, if it would please the Lady Adzuma, and her mother, to look upon our holiday doings.

ADZ. Oh! I long to see them.

WAT. Why, go then, Adzuma! and thou, too,

Okkâsan! I would myself conduct you, but that I hold, to-morrow, the palace-gates.

ADZ. We thank you frankly, Sir! Assuredly we will go.

SAKA. So! that is well—very well! I shall be the best paid messenger in all the City if my errand has brought you pleasure. Now will I take worshipful permission. *Sayonara!*

ALL. *Domo!* we greatly thank you. *Sayonara!*

[*Exit* SAKAMUNE.

[*A noise of something falling is heard within.*]

KOROMO. *Anôné*, Girls!

What have you, heedless, broken?

O TAMA *entering, agitated.*

TAMA.   Madam! Nay,
'Twas not our heedlessness! The effigy
Of Buddha from the *tokonomâ* fell down
And struck a gilded scabbard of my Lord
Out of the sword-rack. All is since made good.

WAT. [*laughing.*] If we had enemies, 'twere ominous !

    There be some fearful folk would burn for this

    A sheaf of senko sticks ! Come, we'll to food :

    The luck of men lives in the deeds of men.

ADZ. I think that, too. If hearts be true and fast,

    Ill fates may hurt us, but not harm, at last.

END OF ACT THE FIRST.

ACT II.

SCENE I.

An open public place in Kyoto, upon which abuts a broad newly-built bridge, of red lacquer and gilding. The bridge and neighbouring buildings are gaily decorated with national flags and painted lanterns. Crowds of citizens, in various dress, throng the approaches, which are kept by armed men.

Enters SAKAMUNE, *apart; in full Samurai costume.*

SAKAMUNE.   What is't the grey-beards mean by

"happiness"?—

Time was I thought no peace could be, no joy,

Outside the amber arms of Adzuma ;

That all the days of all my richest years

Would be well pawned to buy one night with her,

Spent in a million kisses on her mouth.

But now another joy ! a different joy !

The hunter's, not the lover's—yet as great,

Oh, greater, keener, deeper ; tingling more

The vigilant sense—for I shall see to-day

Destiny dance while I do pipe.   He—she—

Will blindly meet, eagle-hot Morito,

And subtle, lovely, snake-bright Adzuma

Whose beauty—will she, nill she—draws men's
    hearts

As on a bank in Spring the *mamushi*

Brings round her shining coils the dazzled birds.

What's after, I will heed : enough to-day

The snare's spread, and here comes my witless prey !

Enters Morito, *armed, and splendidly apparelled.*

Morito. Is all well-set ?   Are our soldiers posted ?
Have the roadways for the procession been sprinkled
with fresh sand and flowers ?   And the upper rooms
of the houses,—are they cleared of such as would dare
to stand higher than the Son of Heaven ?

SAKA. All the worshipful commands have been fulfilled.

MOR. Bare thy bright sword, then, Sakamune, and lay it across thy knee. Good lieges, all, *Shita ni oru!* Down upon your faces, quick! for the Majesty of Japan cometh.

[*The populace prostrates itself, and the Imperial Procession enters by the bridge; the Emperor riding in a gilded and painted kago, borne by footmen, fantastically attired; the Ladies of the palace, Court Nobles, Samurai, Attendants, Dancing Girls, &c., &c., following. Banners, hatamochi, &c., &c.*

[*A troop of young Girls dance the Echigo-jishi, with accompanying song and chorus.*]

CHORUS.

A junk came in with silks and spice,
Oh, the land of Japan is long!
My lover is hoeing the rows of the rice,
What shall we sing for a song? &c., &c.

[*At the departure of the Imperial train, the citizens raise loyal cries of " banzai! banzai!" (" May you live ten thousand years!") and, amongst the departing crowd,*

ADZUMA and her Mother, with their attendants, are seen entering their kago, to return home; and presently disappear by the bridge. SAKAMUNE *and* MORITO *remain alone.*]

SAKAMUNE. Come, my Lord Morito! It is well performed! Deign now to wash the dust of the vulgar from thy throat with a cup of red-fish saké, in my quarters.

MORITO. Sakamune! Sawest thou yonder Lady?

SAKA. What Lady, Trifler!

MOR. Why, her! her!—that most lovely woman who passed hence a moment ago in her chair?

SAKA. Nay, indeed, I saw none. Yet, again, that is false, for I saw scores, hundreds! *Naruhodo!* Every petticoat in the City was out upon us, I think, to gaze at the show.

MOR. *Aho!* nonsense! This one was to all the others as the full moon to a paper-lantern, as the white crane on Arashiyama to the sparrow in the bamboos; as, as, as—

SAKA. Good Morito! hath a flash from some black
eye pierced at last that corselet where an enemy's
point could never yet find its way? We thought you
proof against such light assaults.

MOR. If thou didst not mark her, it matters not.
But I must know her name, and house. I will ride
after them. Take back the soldiers for me, and bid an
officer lead my horse to the lane of the persimmon-
tree, for she passed thereby.

SAKA. *Kashi komarishita!* I obey! [*Aside*] Now
fluttereth my foolish eagle straight to his poisoned meat!

[*Exit* SAKAMUNE.

MOR. [*alone.*]

Have I my selfsame eyesight, reason, will?

Am I that man who this morn buckled on,

Over a careless heart, breast-piece and belt

Whose tough steel hardly keeps the beat of the
heart

From bursting them this hour? Oh She! but
She!

Was ever such form seen, such heavenly grace,

Such eyes of loveliest light beneath a brow

So even-arched, so smoothly shadowing back

Into that twilight, where the black silk hair

Shuts in the soft fair face? Yet 'twas not
    that!

Something beyond her glorious beauty drew.

Where have I seen her? In what spot before

Were we encountered? Nowhere!—Once be-
    held

Would be to be in mind for aye. What voice

Whispers me, then, that she is Destiny?

I rave, and waste my words: but I must go

Whither she goes, be it for weal or woe!

                      [*Exit* MORITO.

             END OF SCENE I.

4

ACT II.

Scene 2.

Back gateway of Adzuma's *house.   People, of various
classes, passing and repassing.   A* Fisherman, *with
his tubs, comes out from the entrance of the house,
as* Morito *approaches.*

Enter Morito.

Morito. Here she went in.   How may I discover
her name ?   Ah! doubtless, this simple fellow will
know it.

> *The* Fisherman, *while repacking his tubs, and
> adjusting his yoke, sings :*

> " *The spot where one may hear
>   The nightingale sing clear
>   Is three ' ri ' from the saké-shop
>   And bean-curds not too near !* "

Mor. *Oi, ryoshi !* hast sold all thy fish to the
mistress of this house that thou chirpest so merrily ?

Fisherman. Your pardon, Danna !   Oh, your high

forgiveness, most worshipful Knight ! I spied not the august presence. My bones are become as water for such boldness.

MOR. Nay ! there is no offence.

FISHER. That is by reason of your Honour's goodness. Why ! there be knights, lording it up and down our city now, with two swords sticking out of their belts, would hack a poor man to little pieces, as I slice a *tai*, if they liked not his song.

MOR. The Emperor's justice should be done upon such.

FISHER. *Naruhodo !* Kind Lord, it is far from the mouths of the poor to the ears of the Mikado. As for justice, we are like the peoples of the sea. The great fish eat the little fish, and to splash too much only makes the other big ones come. Our best safety lies in silence, and the shallows.

MOR. How, the shallows?

FISHER. I mean, worthy Sir ! to be one of a million minnows in a finger's breadth of muddy water. Thus may a poor man live, perchance, until such time as he doth die. Shall I bear a fresh fish, Sir, to your honourable abode?

Mor. Thou shalt earn the price of a whole tub-full of *tara*, if thou wilt truly answer a question. Hold up thy hand ; here be silver *bu*.

Fisher. *Domo !* 'tis a week's good fish-selling to me. I will tell thee as much truth for this, as ever honest words can compass.

Mor. Whose house is this?

Fisher. Why, everybody knows that much ; 'tis the *yashiki* of the Lord Wataru Watanabe.

Mor. Didst thou mark a lady enter in her litter, even as thou camest forth ?

Fisher. Truly I did. 'Twas Wataru Sama's wife, the lady Adzuma. And a most gentle, and a most noble, and a most worthy lady she is ! 'Tis a piece of sunshine to encounter her on the way, or to sell even an *iwashi* into her hands. Nay, if she buy not so much as a single *awabi* from me, I am always richer by the sweet words of her mouth.

MOR. I thank thee! Go thy ways in peace, and Kompira Sama, the god of fishing-nets, send thee customers.

·FISHER. I would they might all be like thee. Then would I let flat-fish and shell-fish for ever alone, and sell only the truth. Truly, it is a good commodity for the markets. Worshipful Knight! I take very humble leave.

MOR. Fare thee well.   [*Exit* Fisherman.]

Adzuma! Adzuma! She, then, is this Star of women—the daughter of my aunt Koromogawa, whom, as I do remember, my old guardian, Dosen, sought for me in marriage; wedded now to Watanabe, my friend and my fellow-knight. Here therefore doth Honour stay my steps. Yet, ah, her face, and her form! Ah, to know she is now within those lattices, desirable as Heaven, dearer than life—but, since all this is so, farther removed from me than the moon from the bird of the night who cries to her.

Enter KAMEJU.

KAMEJU. Are you here, dear Lord! They seek you all over the city.

MOR. Good Kameju! do you know this gate?

KAM. Very well. It is the gate of Wataru Watanabe's house.

MOR. Call it not a house. 'Tis a treasure-shrine that holds a golden goddess; a shell that shuts in a most priceless pearl! I have seen enter here, just now, Kameju, one that has taken with her the heart out of my bosom, the peace out of my days, the strength out of my sword, and well-nigh the honour out of my knighthood. Oh! Kameju, I have seen Adzuma, who should have been my wife.

KAM. You know I love you, Morito.   Long since,

    My father Dosen, dying—to whose care

    Lord Yasuhira left you—spake, at brink

    Of that world whence our still ones speak no more,

    Son Kameju! there is thy liege, thy chief,

Thy breast - brother, thy charge! See that thou giv'st

Core of thy heart, and spirit of thy soul,

Strength of thy arm, and service of thy blood

To Morito Endo, as thy father gave,

Till death unbuckles this my blade from thee.

And, Morito! I have given ;—and I give.

MOR. Right well I wot, brave Kameju and true!

KAM. So shall you better bear me, saying this :—

All deadly as is sweep of steel, and dark

The chance of battle to the soldiermost,

I had liever see you, sweet Lord! thick beset

With thirsty, sparkling swords ; encompassed in

By reek and rattle of a losing fight—

So I were there—than standing safe and sound,

But love-smit, at the door of Adzuma.

MOR.—Your reasons, my Kameju!

KAM.   Half, my Lord,

Are reasonless : the chill that steals the heat

Out of men's veins, when secret shadows pass,

When nameless perils creep: the sense we have—

Keenest for what we love, and quite outside

Work-a-day wit—of some twist in the path

Which leads to woe and fate.   I shall not fright

Morito with what's womanish.   Well, then,

Be my plea thus: here thou and Duty stand

Friends yet, and nobly linked; thy fair days
    smirched

With nothing misbecoming, thy young name

Writ splendid on the scroll of chosen youth,

The Emperor's trusted.   For those eyes of hers,

Those arms of hers, those beckoning breasts of
    hers—

(Which, being given, are no more to give)—

For one of many a fair one in this world

(This one not yours to have)—wilt set all by,

And let them write you down the Knight that sold

Fame, name, and virtue for a plundered bliss?

Mor. Your words are strong.   So is her loveliness.

Kam. Who brought you hither; was't the Samurai?

Mor. She brought, Adzuma brought! The man you
mean

Never so much as marked. On sight of her—

Like whose delightful beauty in this world

Nothing hath been, or can be,—I was fain

To follow, as the leaf rolls with the wind,

As the stream hastens where the valley slopes.

I had no will save what the green sea hath

Obeying the white moon.

Kam.   Oh! be thyself—

Morito Musha Endo. Did she note

The trouble that her fair face wrought on thee,

This lady?

Mor.   Not a whit! her modest eyes

Kept the ground meekly, curtained off from all

By veil of long-dropped lashes.

Kam.   Come away,

Dear Master, and forget! A war is toward,

The Palace keeps a charge of note for thee:

Nothing's yet done amiss! Think that you see

Your Father's spirit softly from his tomb

Win you to come, laying his hand in yours ;

While I, this other hand, thy henchman true,

Humbly constrain. Come ! Do what none else dares,

Make thy proud heart yield—conquer Morito !

MOR. (*gloomily.*) What hast thou in the sword-bag,

　　　Kameju ?

KAM. I did forget.　I hold a message here ;

Wataru sent it.　At the gaming-bout

Last week you played too rash ; you lost a fief

To Sakamune, and, for present lack

Of coin, you pawned your sword, the Bizen one ;

'Twas not well done, dear Lord : you know that too !

Of this heard Watanabe, so he took

Gold in a bag, and bought the good blade back :

'Tis here, and with it, a scroll.

MORITO *reads*—

" To the very true Knight and his Friend, Morito

Endo, Wataru Watanabe sends this, asking pardon for

too bold a good-will,—his sword, to wit. 'Tis too rare a piece to be in any hands save those which have oftentimes wielded it manfully. The sender craves leave still to live Lord Morito's creditor, until such time as he be weary of giving Wataru pleasure, or luckier at the hazard.''

    [MORITO *turns away impetuously from the door*
      of ADZUMA.]

MOR. Hold fast my other hand ; I'll go with thee !

END OF SCENE 2.

ACT II.

Scene 3.

A Banquet-room in a Tea-house, opening on a Garden. Many high officers and Samurai seated upon the mats, drinking saké, and conversing. Dancing girls perform, with music, singing, &c. Painted lanterns and lamps illuminate the Banquet-room and Garden. MORITO, SAKAMUNE, KAMEJU, *and the* LORD OF IDZU *are among the company, with* HOJO, DOI, *and* ADACHI, *all Samurai.*

HOJO. I tell you the old days were the good days. It was merry in Japan before we fetched in from China the outlandish letters and ways.

DOI. Oh, a cup of saké with you, Sir! You are augustly right! The good old times went out with the Shinto times.

LORD OF IDZU. Yes, and the worst is that the pretty women have all passed away with the ancient poetry,

faith, and manners. Minamoto Genji was well ad-
vised to spend his rainy nights railing at the ugly
faces of our modern Japan girls.

SAKAMUNE. O Yuki! [*to a Waiting-maid*] fill up
again my Lord of Idzu's *sakazuke*, and let him see
your black eyes sparkle over the rim of it.   He will
perchance think better of his land then.

L. OF IDZU. Oh, she is all very well for a *maiko*.
But where are gone the famous beauties of Kyôtô?
Who is there now left to match Inishiyi with the
moon-face, or Soto-öri the desire of her day, or
Komachi, who wrote the verses, and was so beauteous that people bought the mirrors into which she
had looked, to get dreams from them?

SAKA. Think you there are none such now?

L. OF IDZU. I say it, Sir! Here sit I, a Hokumen
of the Court, that hath two swords, and am of repute;
yet her Ladyship my wife!—well, she hath not indeed
six fingers, and is not exactly shark-skinned; but,
since she hears me not, I will honestly tell you, she

hath the eyes of a monkey, the nose of a fox, and the mouth of a frog.

ADACHI. Truly, in old times a great nobleman had better fortune.

SAKA. She is doubtless an excellent Lady in the dark, and a good blade mends a bad scabbard. It won't do, however, to tell us that Kyôtô holds no perfect beauty while Wataru's wife dwells in the city.

L. OF IDZU. Is she so fair?

SAKA. Nay, ask Morito. He galloped away from us all, last week at the Bridge, only to get a second look at an angel he had spied, which angel, I heard, was Wataru's wife.

HOJO. I have seen her; and truly she is of a rare comeliness. Wataru's destiny is to be envied. But a most holy Lady! Oh, she hath no eyes except for her husband, and goes not abroad once in a moon, save to pray at the shrine of Kwannon, or to write poetry to the plum and cherry blossoms.

SAKA. She is fair enough. But she is only a woman, after all, like the rest. Who wants may have, if he only knows the right road.

HOJO. What are you saying, Sir Samurai? She hath a husband whom. she adores. Dream you she is of the flesh that makes a *geisha* or a *joro?* Why, *naruhodo!* you set us laughing.

SAKA. *O warai nasaruna!* Don't laugh till you know! I am saying what is true. The woman is well enough: I speak naught against her, specially since Morito has cast his eyes that way. But her mother Koromogawa possesses an extremely base mind. While Adzuma was yet unpromised many a good man sought her for wife; but Koromogawa spurned them all, rejected even our noble Morito, looking about for a rich husband, with plenty of rice-bags and gold *koban.*

HOJO. You have drunk too much saké, Sakamune.

SAKA. Nay! I am talking sooth. Forgetting justice and shame, she sold her pretty daughter to Watanabe;

and she would sell her over again to you, my Lord of Idzu ; or to Morito ; if there were only money enough forthcoming to gild the palm of the old bargainer.

MOR. [*starting up, and half drawing his sword.*] That is a lie, Sakamune ! And, were it not a lie, what intend you, to speak so before this honourable company of one who was my father's sister? It is much if I do not smite you.

L. OF IDZU. Morito, good Morito ! sweet Lord Morito ! be patient ! He is thy friend, and only a little drunk. Remember, if you draw point from sheath, a Samurai's sword cannot go back without blood upon it.

[*They succeed in restraining* MORITO.

SAKA. I was to blame ; I lay my head at your feet, Endo Morito ! The wine had loosened my tongue too much. I was a fool to forget that one like your worship bears an aunt no grudge for discarding him as a breeder does a half-bred stud-horse. It is not well, I see, to be faithful to friends. If you are angry, take my head ; I will not defend it.

Mor. Nay! but thou shalt not say Adzuma hath a price.

Saka. Oh, I doubt not she herself is innocent enough. I was incensed against her mother for despising you. If it is for that you would kill me, strike! I will not even lift up my hand.

L. of Idzu. We think he meant no wrong, Morito!

Saka. How should I mean wrong to Morito Endo, the best of all my friends? If you forgive Koromogawa, forgive me also. I was to blame; I beg forgetfulness.

Mor. Why, then, let it be forgotten. I think, indeed, thou art honest. I am over-quickly moved. Thou, too, shalt pardon my hot blood.

L. of Idzu. *Sa, sa!* this is well! And now let us walk under the stars, and cool our heads. There was never trouble yet between good fellows, but some woman's name brewed it. *Sa ! sa ! sa !*

[*Exeunt Omnes.*

End of Scene 3.

5

ACT II.

SCENE 4.

A Garden-room in ADZUMA'S *house.* WATARU *and* ADZUMA
together.   She is perusing a Chinese book.

WATARU. What read you, Sweetheart?

ADZUMA.   Oh, a foreign scroll

About a far-off land,—quite far, I think,

Where, when they would adjudge some one accused,

The man, or woman, was close blindfolded,

And red-hot shards of brass from the furnace fire

Being then scattered in a Temple-ground,

This he, or she, arraigned, must bare-foot walk

In the fierce labyrinth of that ordeal.

WAT. A dreadful test!   And, if the naked feet

Touched the hot brass?

ADZ.   Then that was guiltiness;

And guiltlessness showed only from good luck

To thread the perilous pathway harmlessly.

WAT. I hope just Heaven would guide the true feet safe.

ADZ. Ah, if it did ! but I must think—alas !

>That, oftentimes, the false foot came through well,
>
>While th' innocent stumbled 'gainst the blazing
>bars.
>
>Life sometimes seems to me like that hard test.

WAT. Wherein, my Pearl !

ADZ. Because,—tread as we will,

>With never so much heed, the path of the years,—
>
>Fate, or our foes, or relics of old faults
>
>Sow the way with so many snares for us.
>
>Oh, dost thou deem that gentle Heaven, indeed,
>
>Would find a safe road 'mid the fires for those
>
>Whose feet were clean of wrong ?

WAT. Surely I do ;

>At last—far-off—nothing befalls the good
>
>Save good.   That I hold firm.

ADZ. If you did see

>My feet burned by the brass ?

WAT. Why, I should know

The dull brass blundered, though a thousand
    tongues

Called thy hurts justice.

ADZ.   Dear and loving Lord !

Hold fast to that !   Go you on guard to-day ?

WAT. 'Till th' afternoon.

ADZ.   Then shall I—by your leave

Ride with my mother to the holy shrines,

And pray the goddess that she keep you well,

Nor weary yet of granting Adzuma

Comfort and courage of Wataru's love.

END OF SCENE 4.

ACT II.

SCENE 5.

The Court-yard of the Hase Temple of the Goddess Kwannon, at Kyôtô, showing front of the Temple, with steps leading to shrine; the praying-rope, and bell; the tank of purificatory water, &c., &c.

Enter MORITO *and* SAKAMUNE.

MORITO. To what end dost thou bring me hither?

SAKAMUNE. I will answer that anon. I vexed you sorely at the Tea-house lately. I am sorry for it.

MOR. I was too hot. But thou spakest lightly of one so sweet, that, seeking to forget her, I still ever steadfastly remember. Oh, Adzuma! why did my idle eyes ever fall upon thee?

SAKA. To take pleasure in a fair face. It is what eyes were made for.

MOR. I have forsworn all further seeing of her. I have received kindness from her husband, who is a gallant and worthy knight; and Kameju says there is no Lady in the land more cherished by her Lord, or happier in her chastity. Oh, that the wars would come again! I would find peace in the front of them.

SAKA. One can be a soldier without dying, and lover without sighing. Adzuma, thou should'st know, belongs to thee by right.

MOR. How sayest thou that?

SAKA. You will draw blade on me if I tell the truth.

MOR. No! no! 'Twas when you spoke ill of my kinswoman before those saké-bibbers.

SAKA. And if I speak ill of her again?

MOR. Oh, say your say.

SAKA. I am foolish to be so friendly, but you shall hear. There is none oweth more to you than your Aunt Koromogawa. She owed you Adzuma, and cheated you out of payment.

MOR. If I thought that!

SAKA. If you thought that, would you sit tamely

down, and suffer the lily planted for you to bloom in another's garden. You—named *hokumen* at twenty— would you let the fox eat what was meant for the tiger?

MOR. No! no!

SAKA. You have seen Adzuma. You know what has been lost—the Jewel of her time; the Star of women; the fairest spouse that ever lay on a man's breast. But if you have sworn patience, why should I speak more?

MOR. Nay, go on! go on!

SAKA. Well, then, Koromogawa, I say, owes everything to your father. She was poor, friendless, and the daughter of a concubine, praying daily to the goddess for a husband. One night she fell asleep in the Temple and dreamed that Kwannon appeared, and bade her take the *haori* from a woman slumbering beside her. She awoke, and saw, indeed, a lady sleeping near, from whom she stole the garment, and departed. On the road a knight was riding, Jiro Yasuhira, who looking in her face, courteously saluted her, and said: "I had a dear wife, who is dead: and

I have sworn never to take another, until I found one exactly resembling her in countenance and figure. Last night I dreamed I should encounter such an one dressed in a blue *haori*, and, in truth, you are just like my lost wife.'' Upon this Koromogawa confessed what she had asked from the goddess, and how she also had dreamed ; after which, thinking it all the decree of destiny, they went to Oshû together, and Yasuhira took her for wife.

MOR. 'Twas that same Lord who slew the great white eagle ?

SAKA. That same ! Well ! very happily dwelled they together, until they came again to Kyôtô, and then a little thing turned out for Koromogawa a large matter.

MOR. It is often so ; *naruhodo.*

SAKA. A tame dove, pursued by a kite, flew for refuge into Koromogawa's litter. Having rescued and returned it, the mistress of the dove invited your Aunt to come within and take repose ; and she was hospitably entertained by this Lady, who was none other than Shiraito, the wife of Endo Morimitsu, your mother. Growing friendly, your Aunt told all the story of the dream, and of the blue *haori* which she had stolen ; and what shame she still felt, though it had obtained her a husband ; so that — spake she, " I would give a thousand *ryo* to find the owner, and restore it."

MOR. That is not like the bad spirit you alleged.

SAKA. Oh, it is to you alone that she is so evil. Shiraito enquired if the garment was of blue silk, with gold chrysanthemums upon it, and Koromogawa answering "Yes," they bade a servant bring it from the litter ; whereupon, steadfastly regarding it, Shiraito exclaimed, " That is my *haori !* I was she who slumbered in the Temple ! "

MOR. Is this all certain ?

SAKA. Oh, it is true. Koromogawa was both re-joiced and ashamed. But your mother comforted her, saying it was the way and will of the Mi-Hotoke, and your father, Morimitsu — entering just then — made her also courteous cheer. Presently, observing the silver dagger which she had laid aside, he asked: "Whence got you this?" Koromogawa replied, "It was the keepsake of my mother, from my father, when he sent her away." "Right well I know it," said Morimitsu, "it was the parting gift of my father to his concubine, and you are my younger sister! How wondrously have we met! I see, indeed, in you the features of my sire." Presently, in came Yasuhira also, having found out where his wife was entered; and they all made good cheer together, and drunk the "three cups" of relationship.

MOR. 'Tis very strange!

SAKA. Afterwards they lived affectionately in one place, and thou wast born of Shiraito, and afterwards Adzuma of Koromogawa. So it was designed by your father and uncle to marry you to your cousin. But Yasuhira died, and Morimitsu too, and the Lady Shiraito. Your aunt alone survived; and Dôsen, your guardian, when you came to age begged Adzuma from

her for your wife. Now 'tis certain she should have
given her.

MOR. Why, I think that, too.

SAKA. It was a vile thing, and a wrongful—I say—
to set thee aside; son of her brother, who had
wrought her such benefits. Adzuma was bestowed
on Watanabe for his gold, and his great estates—
but she was thine by will of the dead—and thou didst
but desire thine own when thine eyes fell lately upon
her loveliness. Howbeit, since thou hast now resigned
her, our priests will praise thee, if not our soldiers.

MOR. This is new to my ears. To all the devils
with the praise of the priests! I am not he whom
any one can wrong without paying for it.

SAKA. Nay! but Kameju hath told thee how
sweetly they dwell together — what love-beds; what
warm times; what secret comforts Wataru hath with
thy lost wife.

MOR. Hold, Sakamune! or I shall strike thee, whom
I should rather thank. Doth Adzuma know of this?

SAKA. Not one whit! They have kept it very heedfully from her and from thee. Had she once seen thee, Watanabe would soon find her kisses grow colder. The bond of past existences is strong!

MOR. Would that I might yet again gaze upon her sweet face!

SAKA. Art in earnest? dost then, indeed, desire that?

MOR. As dry throats desire water; or blind eyes light; or dying men breath.

SAKA. Why, turn thee round, then, and look who repairs hither to prayers. I brought thee here, believing she would come.

Enters ADZUMA, *with her Mother and Attendants, not perceiving* MORITO *and* SAKAMUNE. *She takes water from the Saikai font, and, washing her hands, ascends the temple-stairs, sounds the prayer-bell, and stands awhile praying before the shrine, with head bowed, and clasped palms.*

MOR. (*watching her with a rapt air*).

Thou marvel! thou fair joy!

Framed of delightfulness and finished sweet

From brow to foot with what's desirable !—

Thee they have stolen from me !   And, what's left ?

What's left—having seen such loss—but desperate
  will

To win thee back, though twenty furious swords

Deny ; though gods forbid ; though fates forecast

Sorrow, and horror, and the end in shame ?

What's left—in all the lesser things on earth

Ambition, honour, greatness, pride of praise,

Pleasures of life, joy of glad battle, gold,—

Save dust and ashes, matched with that one gain

Of one good moment in those heavenly arms ?

They   have   stol'n   thee   from   me,   star-bright
  Adzuma !

But I'll have back my treasure, if I thrust

Souls to perdition for my wrongful right !

ADZUMA *now descends, with her Mother ; and, observ-*
  ing SAKAMUNE, *they salute him.*

SAKAMUNE. Good morrow! noble Ladies. To your

    prayers

    The Gods must listen. [*To* KOROMOGAWA] 'Tis

    your kinsman here,

    Lord Morimitsu's son. [*To* ADZUMA] Fair

    Adzuma,

    This is your husband's friend, Sir Morito ;

    The best sword of our Court.

ADZ.   *Hajimemashite !* *

    I am much honoured to encounter you.

MOR. I pray you, at this first you see of me,

    To hold me in your kindness.

ADZ.   I, in yours

    Would rather ask. My husband's friend must be,

    In simple sequence, friend of Adzuma.

MOR. I am happy with but that one word from you.

    Come you with Lord Wataru, oft, to Court,

    Cousin—and friend ?

---

* The Japanese word at a first introduction.

KOROMOGAWA.   Nay ! we are stay-at-homes,

Good Nephew, getting news of your great world

As it sifts through the *shoji*.   Pardon us

If we crave leave : our little household waits.

MOR. Farewell !

> [ADZUMA *and* KOROMOGAWA *walk aside with their attendants.*

So have I seen Heaven's gate-way gleam again !

SAKA. Gate with a key ! Didst thou not mark her look ?

She would have tarried, but the mother drew.

> [*Exeunt* MORITO *and* SAKAMUNE.

> [ADZUMA *and* KOROMOGAWA *come forward to take departure.*

ADZ. Oh ! Mother, in my veins I feel a thrill
As if my blood iced.   What is ill with me ?

KOROMO. Let us haste homeward, Daughter ! This is ill,

And happens not, except by Fate's hard will.

END OF ACT THE SECOND.

ACT III.

SCENE I.

The Gateway of a "Yashiki," or city mansion in Kyôtô.

Enter MORITO *and* SAKAMUNE.

MORITO. Will you still say she cast eyes of pleasure upon me?

SAKAMUNE. What else? what else?

MOR. Since I heard the truth of Koromogawa's ungratefulness I bear another and a more angry mind.

SAKA. She owed you, for your father's kindness, not Adzuma only, but her own good name, her happy days, her easy life.

MOR. That is so indeed. Except for my mother taking her as sister, she was a robber of apparel in a temple.

SAKA. And that is a crime for the executioner.

MOR. I have her thus at my mercy.

SAKA. Yet you would have drawn sword upon me in the tea-house, for saying a lighter thing.

MOR. I did not know. Forgive it! I thought kin must be kind. It was a bitter deed to deny Adzuma to my father's son, when Dôsen asked for her.

SAKA. Never was knight worse used. But Adzuma had no part in it.

MOR. Would it have fallen otherwise, had she known?

SAKA. It must have fallen otherwise.

MOR. Were I but sure of that, the wrath which smoulders in me, would become flaming fury. If she, too, might have desired me, the twenty thousand devils of Echizen shall not keep her from my arms.

SAKA. What would you do, if you had it from her own hand that she saw a better man than Wataru the day she met you in the Temple?

MOR. She will never go to that.

SAKA. But if she make you know it, so that blind eyes might read the book of her heart?

6

MOR. How mean you? If Adzuma avowed it would please her well that I had Wataru's place?

SAKA. Aye, I say that.

MOR. Why, then I tell thee again hell should not daunt me, nor honour hold me, nor friendship fetter my hand; nor pity stay me for my father's sister, who hath cheated his son. I would pluck Adzuma from Wataru, though I soaked my sleeve in blood.

SAKA. 'Tis the fitting spirit.

MOR. Oh, but you dream.

SAKA. Some dreams come true. Have patience in this great love, which deserveth recompense. She whom thou dost desire, desires you. Give time and place for a woman's wit to work in. Those that cage such bright - feathered birds cannot hinder them from singing through the bars.

MOR. To what end are these words of hope? I shall not even cast eyes on her again. My Aunt will look to that.

SAKA. *Sayo ka?* Wilt thou, this very week, see

her face to face anew ; nay, touch her robe, drink perchance from the same cup with her ?

Mor. Ask rather whether the famished would eat. I am mad to sit beside her once more.

Saka. Be patient, then. Wataru comes back soon from Nara, with treasure of the Emperor. Afterward falls the feast in the Maple Gardens, when folks go to gaze on the bright colours of the autumn. If I know of a surety that Adzuma will be there, ask me not how. For thy sake I adventure much.

Mor. Thou art a faithful friend. We will go to the Maple Gardens.

[*Exeunt* Morito *and* Sakamune.

END OF SCENE I.

ACT III.

S C E N E 2.

Garden of ADZUMA'S *house, with Pavilion opening upon
it.* ADZUMA *is sitting upon the mats there with her
maids,* O YOSHI *and* O TAMA.

ADZUMA. Our bravest garments, Girls! We'll not be
    shamed

    Even by maple-leaves. To-morrow falls

    The great feast in the groves of *momiji*

    Where all the city flocks to see the year

    Put on its autumn dress, golden and green,

    Scarlet and purple, saffron, russet, rose :

    Ne ? maidens mine! This earth were good as
    Heaven

    If all men lived as those should live who own

    A house to dwell in, so embellishëd.

O TAMA. *Okusâma !* What robe shall we lay for you?

ADZ. The pearl-grey one with *obi* of pink silk

Sown with white stars, because my Lord likes that ;

But you, my Tama !   You, O Yoshi San !

Be splendid like the autumn butterflies,

Like Autumn's self, though 'tis your time of Spring :

Fetch forth such silks, such crapes, such girdle-
   cloths

Jiban, and *kanzashi*, the maple-leaves

Shall flutter out of jealousy.   My girls !

We will be glad and gay.   Wataru comes.

Be sure you take my writing-box and reeds ;

I shall make poetry.

O YOSHI.   Madam, you can

With any that are best.   That last you wrote—

The *uta* of the moon—every one sings.

ADZ. How went it, Yoshi ? play it, if you know.

O YOSHI *sings to her samisen*—

" *Moon of the autumn-sky !*
   Sentinel, silver and still,
   Where are the dear ones that die !
   Is it well ?   is it ill ? "

ADZ. Ah, Yoshi! that was in the sombre mood ·

    Which sometimes comes upon my dreaming string;

    Now all's for lightness—since my Lord returns

    On honoured errand of the Emperor,

    And we'll make sunshine for him in the house

    And sunshine out of doors, if it be scant;

    But, sure, I think a day all blue and gold

    Will paint Takawo for us.   Give me here

    The *samisen :* I'll make a happier strain.

    ADZUMA *sings to her own accompaniment—*   ·

" *I would hide my soul, as the Asajiu*
   In the reeds of Ono's moorlands do ;
      And none should know me, or see :
   But the Asajiu gleam, by their blooms revealed ;
   And the gladness of love in my bosom concealed
      Shines forth in despite of me ! "

    Think you my Lord took strength enough with

      him?

    There's an ill league to travel in those woods.

O TAMA. Dear Mistress ! he is safe. What wicked men

    Would stand to see Wataru's sword flash forth ?

ADZ. I think so, Tama ! though he had but two.

    Besides, I still remember what he said :

    There comes no evil to the man that's good ;

    So is he safe, plated against all harm

    By that which cannot fear, a soul serene

    Doing no wrong, and dreading none.   But I

    Count the slow minutes, when he is not nigh.

                  [Exeunt Omnes.

      END OF SCENE 2.

ACT III.

SCENE 3.

Night-time. A lane of bamboos in the outskirts of Kyôtô.

Enter WATARU *armed, with two attendants.   One carries a package.*

WATARU. Give me the Emperor's packet. I do not greatly like this place at night for those that are upon honest business.

1st ATTENDANT. Methought I spied the shine of a lantern just now, my Lord, in the thorn-bushes yonder.

WAT. Aye! we had done wiser, perchance, to pass with more help through this wolf's mouth. Give me the bag, I say, and look that your swords are free in their scabbards.

[*Noises are heard.*]

2nd ATTEND. Oh, Sir! I am hit in the side with an arrow.

WAT. Stand fast, now, with your backs to this clump. We will make it warm work for the knaves.

[*A rush of armed robbers takes place upon the little party. Sharp fighting ensues, in which one of* WATARU'S *men falls dead, and the other is wounded, while several of the robbers are put hors de combat.*]

1st ATT. Master! Good Sir! look to yourself. My fellow is slain, and I can give you help no longer.

WAT. Lie safe here between my feet. They shall not come at thee, nor at the charge we carry, while this blade can bite. [*He strikes dead an assailant.*] Ha, foul thief! down with thee to poison the wholesome grass with thy blood. Now for another,—and another !

[*He wounds two more, but is very hard pressed, when* MORITO *enters, with an armed servant. They engage the robbers.*]

MOR. *Hott, hott!* A knight of the Court beset, and at long odds! Stand behind me a moment, Sir ! and take your breath, while I carve my swordmaker's name on these scoundrels.

WAT. Nay, but I will stand at thy side, valiant gentleman ! 'Tis a new sword-arm to me to see thee. *Naruhodo !* well struck ! [MORITO *hews a robber down, and the rest take to flight.*] The rogues are all away. They have stomach for no more steel !

MOR. Are you hurt, Sir ?

WAT. Not a scratch, but one of my poor servants is, I fear, dead, and the other sorely wounded. You have saved, Sir ! the Emperor's private letters and treasure, with, what is of less moment, the life of your grateful servant Wataru Watanabe.

Mor. Wataru!

Wat. The same, albeit more scant of breath than is wont with him. Most welcome friend! I beseech you raise your face-piece that I may see the man whom I must henceforth love.

Mor. Be pleased to pardon me. I desire not to be known.

Wat. You are as modest, Sir, as you are brave, which is to say much.

Mor. It is not that, Sir! Indeed I do not deserve your praise. Any soldier would do as I did.

Wat. Came you by hazard, then, upon my one-handed battle?

Mor. By hazard only, Lord Wataru; I and my servant were returning to the city.

Wat. Had you dropped from Heaven, it could not have been more timely.

MOR. I am glad—and sorry! Beseech you, let me pass unquestioned. The way is safe now, and I will send those who shall succour your man.

WAT. I would dare believe I know your voice, gallant Sir! This is a service, look you, done to the Emperor's Majesty, who will demand of me the name of so worthy a knight. Suffer me to be able to extol you to him.

MOR. Of your kindness hold me excused! By your honourable leave I will now sheath my sword, and be gone.

WAT. Ah! that sword! Surely I remember the hilt! If it be now in its master's hand,—and none other in Japan could so well wield it—you are Morito Musha Endo.

MOR. [*uncovering his face.*] Since you will know me, Wataru, it must be so. I am Morito.

WAT. Now can I tell of thy valour in the Court; as well as of thy knightly silence. If thou must

depart, take with thee my truest thanks. Nay, I pray
thee, if thou goest to-morrow to the Maple-valley,
deign entrance into my tent there, and' drink a cup
of rice-wine with us ; when Adzuma, my wife, shall
speak better gratitude for me. I must now lead my
poor vassal to a shelter.

> [*Exit* WATARU, *supporting his servant.*

MOR. [*wiping his sword blade and slowly sheath-*
> *ing it.*]

Sword ! thou hast paid thy master's heavy debt ;
For that his better part gives thee good praise ;
Sword ! thou hast saved the life which, like a
> stream,
Runs broad and strong between my love and me,
For that my worser part cries curse on thee !
Ah dearest, deadliest beauty ! Hoped I not
That this Lord's wife would fain be fere of mine
Then,—at that minute,—when his heart was large
With generous heat, I would have caught his
> neck

And cried : " Help me ! if I have holpen thee !

Take now my blade and stretch me stark and

    dead

With these less guilty carcasses ; or take

Thy wife away out of my eyes, and ways,

My mind and life, lest I go mad for her."

Then Sword !　I could have worn thee worthy still,

But now what must and will be—must, and will !

END OF SCENE 3.

ACT III.

SCENE 4.

A beautiful valley outside Kyôtô, full of maple-trees, dis-
playing various rich colours of the autumn. A stream
runs down the valley, and on either side of it, holiday-
makers sit in groups, enjoying the air and landscape.
The wealthier and more exclusive have established
tents or booths, by hanging curtains of many hues from
tree to tree, or suspending them upon bamboo poles.
Such an enclosure is seen to the left of the stage, be-
side the stream, with near at hand a maple-tree, under
which the party of ADZUMA *and* WATARU *is lodged.*

ADZUMA. [*lifting the curtain and coming forth, with
her two Attendants.*]

    Oya ! my maids !   I gave you leave to match

    Your prettiest gowns with Autumn's dying dress,

    Yet she outglories you.   O Yoshi, look !

    Would you not say the evening had dropped down

    Out of its sky upon this lovely vale,

    And dyed it sunset-colours ?   Tama, look !

Would you not say—if not the sky of eve

Fall'n, to fix so its purples, pinks, and greens,

Which else are fled before the eyes can feast

Full of their wonder—then, a fairy grove

Planted by peoples of the under-world

Out of the treasures of their under-world

Red gold, and burning brass, and starry gleam

Of silver, and swart copper's sombre glow,

With soft lights, here and there, of sard and jade,

And hard, of coral and of carbuncle ?

How fair it is ! how fresh the air ! how glad

These city folks !

O YOSHI. *Okusâma !* So it is ;

Yet best I like the tender time of the Spring

When the plum covers all our hills with snow,

And afterwards the rosy cherry breaks.

O TAMA. Ah ! but they fade so soon, the blooms of
Spring,

One is so sorry, seeing them, to know

We shall not see them long.

ADZ.   Why, that's a song

" *Hana no irowa,*" and it ends thus—

> *She touches the samisen and sings—*
>
> " *Oh blood-red bloom of the cherry !*
>   *Did you come for pleasure or pain ?* "

O TAMA. I like the Summer best, when no one fears

The wind will plunder what the sunshine gave,

Or Winter's snow come back, for jealousy,

To shroud the cherry boughs.   Then no one goes

One day without delight of scent and tint.

First there's the *yamabuki*, lacquers us

The hill-sides with its gold ; and next there bloom

Rain-roses, silvering them ; and then there's flush

Of pink-eyes in the rice-fields ; and the lanes

Are lighted with the fire-fly buds and flame

Or red azaleas ; and, when those burn down,

Why, there's the *fuji* swinging lilac links

Of sweetness ; and the *kiri*,—sweeter still ;

And there's the iris, floating purple flags,

Zakuro with red coral blooms ; screw-flowers,

Moon-flowers and crane-flowers, and the tiger-tree ;

With lilies—silver, golden, blue and rose—

The *hime-yuri* one, that hath her dress—

Fair ' princess ' as she is—all white and gold ;

And *kanoko*, red-dappled like a deer,

And *ajisai*, which never knows its mind

Whether to blow sea-blue, or pink, or green ;

And lotus cups that come, clean as the dawn

Out of dark mire ; let be green leagues of rice

Waving pearled feathers ; with the *kiku* last

The Emperor's blossom, filling up the year.

Adz. Why, you have made a garden of your words !—

But Tama ! 'tis an Emperor's blossom, too,

The cherry.   Oh ! a thousand years ago

There fell into King Richiu's cup a leaf

Of the wild cherry-flower, and Richiu said :

" This is the fairest flower in all the world,

Cover my kingdom with it ! "

O Yoshi.   Every time

Is good, if we have eyes.

7   .

ADZ.   Yes, every time !

Now, girls ! we'll go within, and warm the wine,

And set the saké-cups.   By turn of the sun.

Wataru will be here, and I've a thought

To make to a verse.

O YOSHI.   Madame ! 'tis strange our Lord

Was so beset last night, and Morito

The knight to help him.

ADZ.   Yes ! O Yoshi San,

Scarce have I slept for joy, since he came back

With dints of wicked weapons on his mail,

But safe, oh, safe !   Grace to the goddess, safe !

Grace, too, to that brave friend who stood by him.

'Tis strange my mother loves not Morito,

But I, until I utter all my heart

Will not touch food.   Oh ! a true knight, I deem,

And goodly—and my cousin.   'Twere not well

We stinted kindliness if he should come.

[ADZUMA *and her maids re-enter behind the curtains.*]

Enter MORITO *and* SAKAMUNE.

SAKAMUNE. 'Tis an odd matter, truly, that you should have lighted last night upon Wataru, in his need.

MORITO. *Iya!* I little wished for it. I was returning with my servant from the hills, thinking much more of his fair wife than of him.

SAKA. *Naruhodo!* Had I been Morito Endo, Wataru Watanabe should have been left to his chances.

MOR. Doubtless, doubtless! You love him less even than I; but I saw not plainly his face in the mêlée, and my blade leaps of itself from the sheath, when it hears the music of steel upon steel.

SAKA. If the thieves had slain him, how easy had been your way to Adzuma's arms.

MOR. Tempt me not to ill thoughts, Samurai! I am desperate enough as it is, and already on the straight road to evil, as I deem, with thee for guide. But I am not yet come to that mind where I could stand by and see a knight of Japan fight alone against half-a-dozen villains.

SAKA. As thou wilt. Know you who sits yonder in that tent with the purple and green hangings?

MOR. Nay! how should I know?

SAKA. There is little need to tell thee; for, look! of herself she cometh forth. Did I not promise to thee another sight of thy Adzuma?

> [ADZUMA *comes out of the tent; and, not observing* MORITO *and* SAKAMUNE, *fastens upon a bough of the maple-tree, according to Japanese custom, a poem written in the native manner upon a long strip of gilded paper, which she leaves there, and then again retires.*]

MOR. (*greatly agitated*).   *My* Adzuma?

Ah! if she were! Again, again, that face

Like nothing in this world, because this world

Owns nothing else so heavenly; that fair shape

Which when I thought I had learned it, line for line,

Shines forth afresh, and lo! I find myself

Marvelling I never knew my star so bright!

My Adzuma! Ah, yes! My Adzuma

If great love had his rights, and kin were kind.

But not to-day, and not to-morrow "mine"

Nor ever, as I think. *His* Adzuma,

Who filched such sweetness from me! His to

    have,

And his to keep, and his to clasp and stroke,

And feast upon, whom I sent home alive

Safe to her out-stretched arms and opened breast

Yesternight; nay not I!—my honester sword.

My Adzuma! No! never, never mine

Except she wills so. Then, death should not keep,

Nor hell, nor any terrors, mine from me;

My Adzuma! Where is that liar fled?

I'll find, and make him fear to mock at me.

    [SAKAMUNE *has withdrawn, to gather up secretly*
       the tanzaku or poem affixed to the maple-
       bough by ADZUMA, *which has been blown*

*away by the wind across the stream, and
picked up by him.   He now returns, taking
the concealed manuscript from his sleeve.*]

SAKAMUNE. Morito gone? that's well!   Let the
proud fool cool, while I look at my treasure-trove.
What have we here?   Adzuma's *uta* to the maple-
leaves.   By the right hand of the Mikado, what neat
characters she forms, and how clever at verses the
pretty little poetess really is!   See how glibly she has
made them run !

He reads—

" The shadows of the maples paint

    The river gold and red ;

  Come quick, dear Love! my heart is faint !

    If spotted deer should tread

This bright brocaded pattern out,—

    Trampling the crystal ford—

Those deer to me not dear would be,

    But brutes I hate, my lord ! "

SAKA. Now, by the thirty-three thousand poets of

Choshiu, she falls ripe into my hands like a dry *kaki !*
See here. It is but to break her last line with one
touch of my ink-brush at that word "brutes," and to
alter a little this letter, and, *zutto !* it reads plain and
blunt "I hate my Lord." Ha! ha! ha! What's
that except to avow to Morito in her own charm-
ing hand, that she is sick of Wataru, and lives but
to have her new fancy cross the stream to her?
Now win I Morito, body and soul, by so small a
revision ! *

[*He takes his ink-case from his girdle and marks
the manuscript.*]

There! that is deftly done! And here comes again
the love-sick knight who shall swallow my philtre.

---

* In the Japanese versions of this story the play upon words,
by which Sakamune effects his devilish stratagem, is untrans-
ferable. Adzuma had written *Fumi na chirashi so,* meaning
"do not disturb by trampling it." Sakamune substituted for this,
Wataru wo itou, which has much the same signification, "I do
not wish you to cross," but also reads, "I hate Wataru," *wataru*
in Japanese meaning "to cross." Thus it was necessary to imi-
tate the trick.

Re-enters MORITO.

MORITO. I sought thee to say plainly I will bear no more of this torment. I go mad upon each new sight of her, but have thrust her now farther away from me than ever, by rescuing Wataru, whom alone she loves.

SAKAMUNE. Art thou so sure of it?

MOR. As I am that thou hast lied.

SAKA. It is more than she herself is.

MOR. Play no more with me, Samurai! I am ill to jest with.

SAKA. Nay, but cast a glance at that.

[MORITO *reads the poem.*]

MOR. Whence hadst thou this?

SAKA. It is the *tanzaku* which you saw Adzuma hang upon the maple-branch. A friendly breeze rent it away, and carried it where I found the precious message.

MOR. How precious?

SAKA. Hast thou eyes? If thou hast, perpend the delicate wit of this. She composes, writes, and then affixes her verses where the wind shall be messenger for her; since, doubt not that she did spy us. If they had fallen into Wataru's hands, small matter! The husband reads past this little mark, and kisses the pretty conceit. But should it come, as it hath duly come, to your undeserving eyes; why, she gives you credit for sense to stay upon this word "brutes," and to read her frank confession, "I hate my Lord."

MOR. *Naruhodo!* There seems something in this!

SAKA. Something! There is everything! there is the woman you love hungering and thirsting for you; casting herself at your feet.

MOR. Sakamune! I will stay here. Nay, if I be bidden, I will go into their tent.

SAKA. You cannot do wiselier. Spake I not well that she needed only time and place?

Enter WATARU.

WATARU. Ah, fair Sirs, you are honourably early! Morito Endo! that I have eaten fish and rice to-day, and drunk saké—a living man with good appetite—is the gift of thy valiancy. Please you—if will serves, and you have gazed enough on the maple-leaves— repair to our booth yonder—'tis that one with purple and green cloths,—and suffer my wife and my mother-in-law to disburden their hearts of the gratitude which will not let them eat.

MOR. Indeed, I merit not their thanks.

WAT. Come and try to persuade them of that; but you will not succeed. I pray you both deign to grace us. We have within a little country feast toward. Nay, but condescend!

MOR. I will come with you.

[*All three enter the tent together.*]

END OF SCENE 4.

ACT III.

SCENE 5.

Interior of WATARU'S *tent.* WATARU *and* ADZUMA *are discovered seated on carpets, entertaining* MORITO *and* SAKAMUNE. *The feast is served after the Japanese manner in small bowls and trays, with saké-cups and pots, a maid-servant kneeling before each guest.*

ADZUMA. I say it again most gratefully, Sir Morito, it was the deed of a true and noble knight.

MORITO. Indeed, you do overpraise me.

ADZ. It cannot be overpraised. My humble words are too poor to tell your rich desert.   ·

MOR. Words from so sweet a mouth would make death itself an easy thing.

ADZ. Oh, Sir! you are courteous as you are brave. Saidst thou, Wataru San! there were still six robbers attacking when Sir Morito drew sword?

WATARU. I did not closely number the dogs, but there seemed too many left for me alone. Nay, 'twas

as friendly, and as timely, and as gallant a help as
ever thou canst declare. Bring hither the saké-pot,
Adzuma! I would fain pledge you, Sir Morito, in a
cup of love.

MOR. Beseech you, excuse me. I do not drink
to-day. I did not see your honour's countenance
in the confusion. I deserve not such high kindliness.

WAT. It was all the more soldierly! For a friend
one risks much; but you say that you knew me not.
Oh! a cup, a cup; *ippai kudasai !*

MOR. Pray you, forgive me! I do not drink
to-day.

ADZ. But, Sir! you will drink a cup with me?

MOR. [*impulsively.*] Aye, Lady, if you poured me
poison !

ADZ. Truly, I love not our strong rice-wine better
than yourself. But we owe you so much !

SAKAMUNE. How much, madam ?

WAT. Well, Samurai! that depends upon the value

to be put on the life of your most unworthy host, with the Emperor's letters and treasure thrown into the account.

MOR. I am to be too much overpaid, Lady, by the honour of drinking from the same cup with you.

WAT. O Yoshi! fill up the wine-cup of your mistress.

> [*In receiving the cup, and holding it to be filled,* ADZUMA *lets it fall and spill.*

ADZ. Ah, my stupidity! Be pleased to grant me august pardon. I cannot tell why my hand should shake so.

> [KOROMOGAWA *calls from within :* "ADZUMA! ADZUMA !"]

Nay, mother ! anon.

> [SAKAMUNE *whispers* MORITO *in the ear.*]

MOR. O Yoshi San! fill again the Lady Adzuma's cup.

ADZ. No, Sir! your gracious forgiveness. I, too, will not now drink. I have a strange feeling at my heart, Wataru. Ask the honourable guests to allow my departure.

SAKA. Our loss will be great, Lady! You are a renowned poetess, and I was dying to enquire if you have wrought any little thing to-day for our city samisens, in honour of the maples?

ADZ. *Oya! oya!* I made, indeed, a very trifling *tanzaku*—a foolish verselet upon the colours of the autumn.

SAKA. If we might but hear it, before you go; it would be better than the cakes and saké.

ADZ. I am ashamed. I wrote such a thing, and hung it on the tree by the stream, but a gust of wind carried it away.

WAT. Then you also, Adzuma - chan! have been robbed, and no Sir Morito near at hand to aid you.

SAKA. Truly, rather it is we who are robbed, Lord Wataru! losing so sweet a song.

ADZ. [*smiling.*] Ah, Sirs, it was not worth so

much as one of the red maple-leaves, which flew over the river with it.

SAKA. The wise wind was of another mind, and stole it away to sing to the maple-trees. Is this also a piece of yours?

[*Taking up a strip of writing.*]

ADZ. It is, Sir.

SAKA. In your own very hand, dare I ask?

ADZ. Even so.

SAKA. May I turn robber like the wind, and take it, in remembrance of this fortunate occasion?

ADZ. Sir Samurai! nothing can be refused to-day to Lord Morito, or to his friend.

SAKA. I humbly thank you.

[KOROMOGAWA, *from within, calls again* "ADZUMA! ADZUMA!" ADZUMA *kneels before each guest, and salutes him with her hands and forehead on the ground: then rises, and passes within.*]

O TAMA [*entering.*] I am to say to the august presence that the *Okusâma* has gone home with her mother. They beg honourable excuses.

MOR. We, too, will now take our leave.

WAT. Nay, but drink! drink!

MOR. Your honourable forgiveness. Already we have stayed too long.

WAT. Well then, at another time. I heartily pray you to distinguish my unworthy house in the city by visiting it.

MOR. I shall come.

WAT. Fare you well! And you, Sir! Come, again, at your august leisure.

[*Exeunt Omnes.*

END OF SCENE 5.

ACT III.

SCENE 6.

A bridge, leading by steps through a cemetery.

Enter MORITO *and* SAKAMUNE.

SAKAMUNE. I say to thee, but for those present, she had embraced thee then and there.

MORITO. Certainly she was much stirred.

SAKA. Did'st thou mark her let fall the saké-cup?

MOR. Yes! and the colour burning in her cheeks at that moment!

SAKA. Yea, but most when I spake of the *uta*, which she made the wind carry to our hands. Oh, she is thine, if thou wilt have her.

MOR. I think so. Almost I think so!

SAKA. It is Koromogawa alone that hinders. Did'st thou not note how she twice looked through the curtains, and twice called Adzuma away? Go to her house, at Toba. Be not denied. Be resolute; be pitiless; be terrible! Tell her what thou hast learned; what thou hast determined. Bid her bring Adzuma to thee there, or abide thine anger, and the shame of thy denunciation as the robber of Shiraito's robe in a holy temple. The penalty of such a deed is to have both hands cut off, and the thief's name erased from the family-line. Go! if thou would'st have Adzuma all thine own—go!

8

MOR. If I would have her ! Samurai ! Yon Dead,

    That keep such settled silence in the mould,

    Lie not more still under their graven tombs

    Than, in my breast, the sense of pity sleeps.

    I will not spare. I will avenge my wrong.

    I have been plundered of a precious thing;

    Hatefully scorned; set by; shorn of a wife—

    Willing, as now I think, to have spent on me

    The treasure of her tenderness, but chained,

    Gagged, cheated, sold to slavery for gain—

    Whose prison I will break. If I would have?

    I tell thee Death, Hell, Danger, shall yield now

    To the awakened fury of my love

    As the thin airs part, and the filmy clouds

    Before the swooping Eagle's stiffened wings.

    They shall bewail who flouted Morito,

    And I will lie with loveliest Adzuma.

                        [Exit MORITO.

SAKAMUNE. Now I have set them fairly at each

others' throats. There will be sport out of it all,

before the end. Meantime here is my pretty Lady's
handwriting, which I have narrowly studied. She
makes her " *I-ro-ha* " very beautifully, and it is hard
to match such fair penmanship, yet I have been at so
much pains, that I do think this love-letter, which I
will deliver to Morito, might pass with Adzuma herself
for her own handwriting. Let us see how it runs :

He reads—

*"I lift to your most honourable eyes this my very
humble letter, believing you the true friend of Lord
Morito Endo. I saw you gather up my tanzaku, and
he will know therefore what I did write at the close of
it. I am not, indeed, so wicked as to 'hate' Wataru,
but I have heard that our parents would have united us
in marriage, and of late I have seen the comeliness of Morito, and have learned his valour; wherefore the heav-
iness of my heart to be separated from him by that husband whom my mother forced me to marry, caused me
to write such a verse. I pray you to let Morito understand this little of my very loving and sorrowful soul."*

So !—holding this, Morito cannot well miss to frighten
Aunt Koromogawa into consent. I am proud, in truth,

of my lady-like writing. Ah! but here comes one of
the few whom I have to fear.

Enter KAMEJU.

KAMEJU. The day to you, Samurai! Where is my
Lord Morito?

SAKA. When I am *omba** to him I will stand ready
to tell you of his comings and goings.

KAM. It suits you to be uncivil. Where is Morito?

SAKA. What if I say I know not?

KAM. I should say you lied. He was with you
here a little while ago.

SAKA. If you knew so much you wasted breath to ask.

KAM. I waste breath, indeed, to ask truth from you,
Samurai! or trust, or honour.

SAKA. Were you of my rank, Heimin! † it is with
tongue of sword that such insolence should be answered.

KAM. Were you of my rank, Sir Sakamune! I
had long ago obliged you to draw that steel which

---

* "Wet-nurse."   † "Peasant."

you defame by wearing. It is your present safety, look you, that I am only the retainer of my master. But I love him, and I serve him faithfully ; and it is sorrow to me and trouble to see him day by day in your evil company. He hath of late lost his gallant spirit, goes melancholy, and cares not for the service of the Court, nor for the manly exercises of a Japanese nobleman.

SAKA. What is all this to me, fellow ?

KAM. Nothing to-day, perhaps. But it is a score I watch, knowing not yet how the account will come forth. Have a care, I bid thee, what thou dost contrive with my Master, and whither thou dost push his feet. Those that love him watch thee, Samurai !

[*Exit* KAMEJU.

SAKA. The meddling peasant ! It would stain a bright blade past cleaning to wet it in such vulgar blood. Otherwise—otherwise !

[*Exit* SAKAMUNE.

END OF SCENE 6.

ACT III.

SCENE 7.

An apartment in the house of KOROMOGAWA, *at Toba, near Kyôtô.* KOROMOGAWA *is sitting with her maids, who are embroidering.*

KOROMOGAWA. Draw the threads thus, Tora San, if you would have your dragon stand forth finely from the silk. What are you doing, O Tatsu?

O TATSU. I am designing birds and trees, *Go Inkyô Sama!* for an over-gown.

KOROMO. This is well; but you must have the proper birds and creatures with the proper trees. Do you not know that the sparrow goes with the bamboo; the lion and the peacock with the peony; the dove with the wistaria; the crow with the pine; and ducks and fishes with the lotus.

O TATSU. I thank you, madam! I will make it so.

Enters a Maid-servant.

Musumé. *Okusâma!* The Lord Morito Endo stands at the gate, asking to speak with you.

Koromo. Beg of him the august pardon. To-day I receive no guests.

Musumé. Your honourable forgiveness! He bade me say he prayed not to be denied.

Enters Morito *abruptly.*

Morito. Nay! but he said that he *would* not be denied. As you see, Aunt Koromogawa, I have admitted myself. Dismiss the serving-girls. I would talk with you alone. [*The* Musumés *all retire.*

Koromo. Do you not even salute me, Morito?

Mor. No, kinswoman! And take heed that none of thy servants eavesdrop, for what I must say is for thy private ear.

Koromo. Thy manner pleaseth me not, Morito!

Mor. It is not meant for liking. Listen! If there

should be one among a man's relations to whom his father showed great kindness, saving and restoring her after a heinous fault, and if she repaid that kindness with slight and despite to the son, were it becoming in that son—a soldier—to restrain his wrath.

Koromo. I do not understand.

Mor. But thou shalt ! Dost thou remember who it was—desolate and disregarded—that prayed long and hard for a husband in the Hase-dera at Kyôtô, and afterwards stole from a sleeping woman there a blue *haori* spotted with chrysanthemums?

Koromo. It was the will and way of the goddess that I should take it. Long ago was it given back.

Mor. Thy crime served thee well, I know—but it was a crime, *Obâsan !* of which the punishment by law is mutilation and degradation.

Koromo. Dost thou dare to speak such words to the sister of thy father?

MOR. I dare, because my father's sister hath wrought me bitter wrong. I dare, because she can atone for it, and shall atone for it; or I myself will denounce her to the justice of the Mikado.

KOROMO. What wrong, Morito? I have feared thee, but never misliked thee before.

MOR. This wrong: you married Yasuhira, and became a well-reputed and happy wife. But you had deceived your Lord when he questioned you, touching your kinsfolk in Kyôtô, and you would have stood declared a liar—as already you were secretly a thief —except for the chance which brought you into my father's house, and the grace shown by Yasuhira and Shiraito to the concubine's daughter.

KOROMO. I have my dagger here. Morito! I will not endure such words.

MOR. Aye, *Obâsan!* That dagger is part of the story. Yasuhira saw and recognised it, as the gift of his father to thy mother, and, freely admitting thee his sister by blood, forgave thy sin and the robe stolen from my mother, Shiraito—for it was she whom thou didst rob—took thee to peace and honour; and died thy benefactor, friend, and brother.

KOROMO. I deny nothing of this, save that my taking the robe was by a dream from the goddess. We must obey Heaven—but indeed I sought long and hard to restore the blue kirtle.

MOR. Dost thou deny that, being left alone, but well-provided, by favour of my dead father, thou didst refuse to me, his son—through Dôsen—the fair daughter thou gladly gavest to rich Wataru?

KOROMO. Yes, but for thy sake and for hers, if thou knewest all.

MOR. How meanest thou?

KOROMO. They that hate thee and me, and have set thee on to this, have not told thee of the old beginnings of thy life, and Adzuma's. They have not told thee of the dreams which brought my lovely child to me from the snakes' bank, and thee to thy mother's womb from the eagle's eyrie. There was between you a destiny of mutual ruin, only to be overcome by virtue, and the mercy of the Compassionate One. I did thee true service keeping Adzuma from thine eyes.

MOR. To the priests and the country-gossips with such folly !

KOROMO. It is no folly. We do not touch the sleeve of another person in this existence, but it imports contact heretofore and mingling fortunes. Morito, I even loved thee. I would have desired that which Dôsen asked ; but the Snake and Eagle must not again meet, and, moreover, my child's heart was already given. The goddess had, of herself, brought together Adzuma and Wataru.

MOR. You lie, my Aunt ! And, if you lie not, I will not now be lulled with nursery tales, like a *chikusai*, a child that smells of milk. If this be true, did not my father know it, who wished Adzuma for me ? You refused her. The unsatisfied longing of spirits holds them from their repose, and these many years Yasuhira's soul hath wandered indignant. Hear me! I love Adzuma! With all my body and my blood I do desire her sweet beauty. With all my wit and will I do seek possession of it. I will not live without her; nor will I suffer thee to live, unless thou dost comply with my demand: Help me to have Adzuma!

KOROMO. Oh, unhappy and unknightly one! Adzuma is no light o' love; but heart and soul the faithful wife of a noble Lord, to whose ears I bid thee, if thou dar'st, speak these base words. Could I be vile enough to fear and to aid thee, she would never be. Thou dost lose thy shameful labour!

MOR. Nay! I know what I ask. Adzuma also desires me.

KOROMO. Though thou slay me I call thee liar, saying so.

MOR. I will show thee sure proof, and to spare, of it. Moreover, she shall herself avow in thine hearing that she loves me only, and that thou didst commit a second great crime, keeping her from my bed.

KOROMO. A second crime?

MOR. Aye, for the first awaits the executioner's knife, upon a word from me in the ear of justice.

KOROMO. Coward, as base as liar!

MOR. I will not kill thee now. I will kill thee if thou dost not call Adzuma hither to meet me in this same room. She shall confirm what I have told thee; and then thou shalt give her to me, or die.

KOROMO. I fear thee not. I can die by my own dagger if what thou sayest were true. But I fear thy evil spirit. There is some miserable plot herein which her truth shall shame. Adzuma shall come hither to-morrow to answer thee, and afterwards it is Watura Watanabe to whom thou thyself shalt answer. Be-gone! lest a knight's widow smite thee on the mouth for her daughter's name. To-morrow; in the after-noon!

[*Exit* MORITO.

END OF ACT THE THIRD.

ACT IV.

Scene I.

A Street, with temple-gate and steps.

Enter WATARU *and* KAMEJU.

WATARU. I like the Samurai as little as thou thyself, Kameju! yet, sooth to say, with no very good reasons for it.

KAMEJU. There is reason enough in the looks and the ways of Sakamune. What mischief he is working with my Lord I have not yet discovered; but Morito Endo is no more himself. He sleeps not, eats not, drinks not, fights not. His war-horse grows gross at the manger for want of use; and since the festival at the maple-trees I have not once seen him string his bow for the practice.

WAT. Thou and I, good Kameju! will arouse him.
A new war is gathering in the East, and we will take
him there. After what he wrought for me and for
the Emperor's treasure, the Court is well disposed to
Morito.

[*Exit* KAMEJU.

Domo ! what spy I here? The crest of my house upon
the bearers, and Adzuma's litter borne so quickly?

Enter ADZUMA *in her kago. Seeing* WATARU, *she
alights, and respectfully salutes her husband.*

WATARU. Whither, in such high haste, my Adzuma?
ADZUMA. Oh, not to pleasure if not where thou art!
My mother sends me word some trouble irks,—
A little ache, I hope—prays me repair
With all the speed I may. One must not keep
A mother long expectant—must we, dear ?—
Even for bribe of blessèd times at home
When thou art there, and this too burning noon
Melts to the purple peace of evening.

WAT. Nay, but be back long ere the evening !

    I have a thing to show thee—ah ! a piece

    Wonderful for its fancy—newly wrought.

    Art thou so hurried, wife ?   List ! there's a hill—

    'Tis done in pearl and ivory on a plate

    Of silver—there's a hill, and on the hill

    An ancient castle ; and the castle's held

    By rebels ; and the reigning Emperor's troops

    Must take it, if they take the place at all,

    Soon ; since there comes an army of relief

    Will raise the siege ; but 'tis of utmost need

    The place be yielded to his Majesty,

    Therefore the question stands, " Have these men

        food,

    Or must they open, starved, if siege be held ! "

ADZ. Yes ; my sweet Lord ?

WAT.   So they send in a spy

    In woman's clothes, young Genjiro, the knight,

    Who enters safe ; and seeks, and hears, and sees

    There's provend but for two days in the fort,

And that such stuff as dogs would sniff and
   leave :

Whom, as he steals back with his precious news,

They mark, detect, unguise—'tis Genjiro !

Oh ! every rebel knows him,—Genjiro,

The best bow of the enemy ! fierce hands

Seize him and thrust him to their rampart-edge.

ADZ. Ah, how I long to see this piece of work !
   What will they do ?

WAT.   Yonder's his tent, his wife,

His comrades, and the friendly, pleasant camp,

All that life means ; and at his back spear-blades

Sharp pricking, and a savage voice which growls :

" Shout ' Friends ! they have taken me ! the fort
   is full,

Victualled for twenty days—best raise the siege ! "

ADZ. Is that what the plate pictures ?

WAT.   Not just that ;

The point's a little later.   Genjiro,

Upon the wall, hears what they say to him ;
   9

Feels the pushed spears prick ; knows that he

    may live

If he will lie, and let his duty go :

But, all too loyal to buy life with shame,

He thunders, '' Ere the week is out they starve !

Keep leaguer still ! '' whereon a sheaf of spears

Pierce him ; but Genjiro has saved his Lord.

That's what the craftsman shows.

ADZ.   Oh, I'll come home

    Quickly to see it.   'Tis a noble thing

    To die for duty.   You had done it, too,

    As well as Genjiro.

WAT.   Adzuma-chan,

    The '' would-dos '' and the '' have-dones '' differ so !

    Yet, an' I loved not honour more than life—

    Aye, more than Adzuma,—I should not love

    Adzuma half so well.   Hasten thee back,

    And see my silver knight rejoice to die

    Where death was duty.

ADZ.   Keep it for me, Lord !

I praise the tale. Like a glad bird I'll come

Whose wings know of themselves the way to
home.

[*Exeunt Omnes.*

END OF SCENE I.

ACT IV.

SCENE 2.

The apartment in KOROMOGAWA's *house.* KOROMOGAWA
and MORITO *are seated together. She holds a letter,
the pretended letter from* ADZUMA *which* SAKAMUNE
has given to MORITO. *She is weeping, and deeply
agitated.*

KOROMOGAWA. Who brought thee this letter?

MORITO. It is idle to ask me that. Thou seest it
is her own. Thou hast thyself said, "This is Adzuma's
handwriting."

KOROMO. That was before I read the shameful
words.

MOR. I care not. Wataru's wife loves me, as thou seest. So thou art twice condemned for the wrong thou didst, denying her for me to Dôsen.

KOROMO. I tell thee she was pledged to Wataru by the will of the goddess, when Dôsen asked her.

MOR. She was given in a dream, but I will have her back awake. With what false pretences dost thou still cover thy ingratitude? If Adzuma be not now yielded to me, when she herself desires it, thou shalt die, and thy name be defamed.

KOROMO. I am not afraid to die, but I am afraid to be dishonoured. Adzuma must answer. I think this letter is a lie, forged by some enemy.

MOR. Wilt thou say so, looking at it? Are these not her own characters, both of the poem and the letter?

KOROMO. *Odorokimashita!* they are very like. Yet it could not; it cannot be!

MOR. But it is!—Why cometh not Adzuma?

KOROMO. I shall wrong her to let her ears listen

to such wickedness. Yet she will come. She will make thee know thou hast fed upon falseness and fancies. Oh, my Daughter! if this shame could be!

Mor. I say, again, it 'is! Adzuma shall tell thee how she loves me. Why comes she not?

Koromo. Even now I hear her dear voice. Oh, would I were a man, and not of thy blood, that, at the first word of her denial, I might strike thee with the scorn of sword-blade.

Mor. Vex me not, shrew! I am dangerous.

Koromo. Aye, to women, Morito, it seems. But thou shalt answer hereafter to those who can do better than weep.

Mor. I shall be ready.

Enter Adzuma, *who makes respectful salutations, and then gazes with troubled countenance on the angered faces of* Koromogawa *and* Morito.

Adz. I feared you were sick, dear Mother! Why is this gentleman here?

Koromo. Do you know him?

ADZ. Oh yes! it was he who brought rescue to my Lord in the lane.

KOROMO. It is he who now brings shame to us, and sin, and the sorrow of wicked words and wishes, and cruel threats to slay and disgrace me, if I yield thee not up to him, away from Wataru.

ADZ. [*starting up to her feet.*] Mother!

KOROMO. I should crave pardon, I know, for speaking so to thee, but thou must hear me—and him.

ADZ. I cannot understand!

KOROMO. How shouldest thou understand? Nor know I in what way least to wound thine ears with the understanding.

ADZ. Away—from Wataru?

KOROMO. Aye!

MORITO. Aye, Adzuma! for I must find my tongue, though thy beauty, at first entrance, hath struck it dumb. I love thee, and do long for thee, as never yet lover longed. From the hour in which I first saw thee upon the Bridge, and afterwards again at the Temple, and yet again at the Feast of the Maples, my heart hath been filled with thee, and my soul sick for thine embraces. Thou wert designed mine by the will of the dead, by secret destinies, by thine own hidden desires ; but this evil woman robbed me of thy love, and gave thee to another. Now, with a sword and a will nowise to be gainsaid, I am come here to claim and take thee. If thou sayest " Yea," as thy pen hath already sweetly promised, and if thy Mother, being assured of thy mind, hinder not, have thou no fear! There is neither danger nor blame that I will not answer and crush. If I am crossed or denied, I will find my way to my purpose in wrath and ruin, and blood.

ADZ. My pen hath promised thee? Morito Endo! I am Wataru's wife !

MOR. By wrongfulness, as thy Mother knows.

ADZ. By rightfulness, as love, and honour, and true faith witness. Oh ! what is all this wild wickedness ?

MOR. With twenty times Wataru's fondness for thee I love thee, Adzuma !

ADZ. 'Tis twice twenty times false! And, were it true, thy disgrace is measureless to tell it, and my shame speechless to hear it said.

KOROMO. Then it is false, Daughter! to say that this letter came to Morito from your hand?

ADZ. What letter, Mother? [*She receives the forged scroll, and slowly peruses it, reading from it at the end.*]

"I pray you to let Morito understand this little of my very loving and sorrowful soul"—

And that signed "Adzuma!" Ah! what enemy has invented against me such impossible sinfulness?

KOROMO. It is not of thy writing, child?

ADZ. Oh, no! no! no! no! no! Could you deem so, Mother? Have *you*, Morito Endo, believed a Japanese wife would be so vile, so false, so wanton?

MOR. Wilt thou deny the characters? Is it not exactly thus thy hand goes?

ADZ. Alas, yes! it is indeed my manner. It is done with a bitter cunning.

KOROMO. You are assured it is false, nevertheless!

Adz. Good Mother, yes! I wrong myself and my Lord to look so closely at the lying scroll. But see now, this ink is paler than I use, and here is a letter not of my habit.

Mor. Oh, Adzuma, Adzuma! will you take back the promise of your eyes, your words, your written mind, because Koromogawa frowns and weeps? Here is your name as none but you yourself can write the precious letters of it. Here is your seal, which only you yourself possess. If you deny this letter, out of fear, will you also deny the *tanzaku*, which the wind blew into my hands?

Koromo. What *tanzaku?*

Mor. This! [*drawing the poem from his girdle.*] Here is what Adzuma wrote, and hung upon a maple-branch at the festival. Read it! See if she did not plainly tell me, " I hate my Lord."

Koromo. [*after reading the poem.*] Adzuma!

Adz. Give it me here, Mother. Ah, yes! that is my writing.

KOROMO. But see'st thou—at the end?

ADZ. I see.

KOROMO. And this is not false, then?

ADZ. No, not this.

KOROMO. And you made the wind your messenger to tell this knight—and all—that you were weary of your husband?

ADZ. Mother! Mother! It is the accursed device of this man, or of some other enemy. Here, at that mark which I never set, an evil hand hath broken the sense of my innocent song, and made the loving, wifely words I wrote rank and guilty as a harlot's.

KOROMO. But the writing so alike! And two of them! And this, you do confess, your own hand.

ADZ. Aye! aye!

KOROMO. And I bethink me, now, how you have lately praised Morito Endo to me; and called him comely and gallant; and how I was forced twice to summon you away from him at the feast in the tent.

ADZ. Aye!

Mor. Oh, it is only the dread of you which forces her to belie herself and her heart. Adzuma! my Desire, my Delight, my Destiny! Fear nothing, and fear none, but give thyself up to thy sweet will and to me!

Adz. Wataru! Wataru!

Mor. Nay, name not him, lest I lose patience.

Adz. Wataru! Lord Wataru!

Koromo. Criest thou to thy husband for anger, or in shame, Adzuma? [Adzuma *is silent.*]

Koromo. Wilt thou have Wataru see these writings? [Adzuma *is silent.*]

Koromo. Adzuma! Hast thou no better speech than barely to call these writings false, which fit so well together, and fall in with thy entertainment in the tent; and thy talk, of late, about this knight; and his own persuasion of thy strong desire for him. [Adzuma *still maintains silence.*]

Koromo. This is sharper than thy disgraced sword, Morito! This is harder than any dishonour thou couldst put on me ! Here, for the house of Yasuhira, begins ruin, infamy, death, unless thou canst better answer, Daughter !

[ADZUMA, *with bowed head, still preserves silence.*]

KOROMO. Thou speakest nought ? Then I call thee " daughter " no more. I call thee strumpet, *Yotaka*, plucker of stranger's sleeves. Ah, thou dishonoured wife ;—thou defamed Lady ! Let me look no longer on thy guilty cheeks and downcast eyes. There is the proper punishment for thy offence writ in the law against the wicked wives that sin. But I denounce thee not to that. Live on with thy *mippu* here, thy fancy, thy knight who makes war upon women, and gathers up love-messages from the gutter ! I disown thee, I am done with thee. Adulteress ! Thus ! thus ! and thus !

[*She strikes* ADZUMA *three times and goes out.*]

MOR. Comfort thee ! this is but a passing spleen.

ADZ. Hold down thine evil voice ! let me be still !

MOR. Now she is gone wilt thou not turn to me ?

ADZ. Aye! I will turn, to bid thee hate thyself.

As I do hate, and scorn—and pity thee.

MOR. I am not used to pity.

ADZ.   Well, begin !

See thy sick honour as my sad eyes see ;

Conceive thy knighthood as my virtue doth

Loathsome, attainted, foul with lust and pride !

Measure thyself by what thou wert, or no !—

Since that was falsely honest—mete thyself

By such brave stature as my husband's worth ;

So learn, how low and petty thou art sunk

That plott'st against his frank nobility.

Mark how, in this hard strait and gathering gloom,

That which thou call'st thy love is vile to me,

And sweet my Mother's anger.   Oh, I praise

The hand which struck the guilty Adzuma ;

If Adzuma were guilty.   Though I see

No way to escape the anguish of these snares,

I pity thee more than myself.   Now, go !

Compassionate thine own state, judging so !

MOR. Didst thou not write the letter?

ADZ.   Why, no! no!

MOR. Nor yet the trick of the verse?

ADZ.   The knave who did

    Laughs at his easy dupe's simplicity.

    I love Wataru to the last live drop

    Of this true body's blood.   Were it not so

    Should I be mad enough to bid the wind

    Puff my shame hither and thither.   Go! thou

        fool!

MOR. Why wert thou silent, when thy Mother cursed?

ADZ. The plot's too deep; no words could do me good.

MOR. I do begin to fear myself deceived.

ADZ. But thy fell folly ruins more than thee.

MOR. I have pushed thee, Lady, to a troublous

    place.

ADZ. Thou hast not wit enough to know how hard.

MOR. Aye! and I have not will to have the wit.

    See now! as here I stand; never before

    So near, so sure; never so deeply drenched

With this strong sea of love, which, from thy form,

Thy face, thy grace, thy wrath, floods and reflows,

And sweeps my soul away—that soul, which

    drowns,

Clutches at thee as sinking sailors will

At what they hold, and will not let thee go ;

Nay, cannot let thee go.   Hark, now !   I swear

Thou shalt be mine ; either by willing love

When I will compensate with tenderness

These terrors ; or because of darker dreads ;

Since, if I have thee not, I'll hold thee up

A scorn-mark, and thy dam a temple-thief ;

And those that called thee honest, shall go by

Holding the nose : Wataru most of all.

                               [ADZUMA *does not reply.*]

MOR. Answerest me not?   [*She is still silent.*]

MOR. I say, answerest me not?

ADZ. [*speaking to herself.*]   If I should tell

    All to Wataru, and he killed this beast,

    His whole life long cold doubt would torture him.

MOR. I cannot hear thee ; wilt thou answer not?

ADZ. Yea ! Yea ! I'll answer. I did meditate.—

There seems no other way.—Truly, it seems

You cannot but be somehow recompensed.—

You have done much for me, have sold your soul

To ruin, ruining me. Well, I must pay

As women pay. Your wild will wills it so.

Who knows? It may be this is destiny.

I yield—I give myself :—it must be thus.

But one condition !—thou shalt slay my Lord.

MOR. Aye, I will slay him.

ADZ.   While I live, and he,

This could not be ; so thou must slay my Lord.

MOR. I'll slay him. Tell me how.

                        Come thou, to-night ;

A little after midnight, to my house.

I shall go back there. When Wataru sups

I'll fill his wine-cups fast, then wash his hair,

And lull him into sleep. His room will be

The easternmost, that gives upon the lane.

I'll set a lamp in it; and, when I hear

Thy foot for certain, I'll extinguish it.

Have thou a care : the serving-men lie thick

In the fore-court.   When thou passest in the dark

Safe to his mat, thou shalt know well his head,

Being moist with washing, and the locks tied back

In the noble's way.   Cut off the head—and go !

And—afterwards—

MOR.   Ah, afterwards—I see

Sweet bliss together, and no fears to mar.

ADZ. Afterwards, as it shall be.   Come to-night !

MOR. Surely I will.   [*Exit* MORITO.

ADZ.   There was no other way !

I never could have laid these plots quite bare ;

He never would have lulled a lingering doubt ;

My mother's honour, life, peace, love for me ;

My husband's name, his trust in Adzuma ;

My own true innocence, go safe this way

And by no other road.   If I should tell

All to Wataru, and this wretch should fall

10

Under his vengeful sword, how would he know

I wrote no wanton word ? how could men part

Mine honesty from fear ? It must be done !

Aye ! I must make him kill me. Killing me

Blindly he sets wrong right. Yet, ah ! I ache,

My dearest Lord ! chiefly I ache for thee

So lonely when my pillow is not there

O' nights—(perchance he'll always keep it by

For thoughts !) But thou wilt know, dear, wilt

    thou not ?

How wholly true I was—all—always—thine.

Yes ! this must be ; Adzuma dead shall free

Adzuma living from all calumny !

END OF SCENE 2.

ACT IV.

SCENE 3.

A street in Kyôtô. A lamp and candle-seller's shop in foreground. The dealer is seated among his goods.

Enter Fisherman.

FISHERMAN. *Komban!* Mr. Lamp-seller, a candle for my lantern, please.

LAMP SELLER. Do you do such a business, *Ryoshi!* that you sell fish by night?

FISHER. *Naruhodo!* one must sell when the fish come; and besides folks like a fresh *tai* or *tara* for their supper. I am even now going to my Lord Wataru's house with some *aji*.

LAMP S. What is this token on your lantern?

FISHER. I bought it for the sign of good-luck, but I am like Kichibei's dog, I cannot read.

LAMP S. What about Kichibei's dog?

FISHER. Well, he was drowned for not knowing his

letters. He was always barking at people, and biting them, until somebody said that if you wrote the China letter for " tiger " in the palm of your hand, and held it out to an angry dog, it would become gentle.

LAMP S. Ha! ha! did they try it?

FISHER. A learned man did, and the dog bit a piece of silk out of his *hakama*, with much of the leg inside it. Oh, it is ill to be without letters, like me and Kichibei's dog. Now what really means my lantern-writing?

LAMP S. It means *Temmei*—" Destiny."

FISHER. Nay! that is well enough for a fisherman !

LAMP S. How so ?

FISHER. *Domo !* See you not we are the very signs and servants of destiny ? Here am I, Kôzô, the hawker, in your honourable shop buying this candle, and there in the river is a fat *Koi*, eating worms. And to-morrow, though we have never seen each other, we shall meet, and I shall catch him, and sell him for half a *kuban*. And all because it was destiny.

LAMP S. So it is! you are honourably right! Fish and men, we cannot escape *Temmei*.

FISHER. For the candle, how much, Danna?

LAMP S. Nay, nay! give me a little ˗ fish, and go thy way.

FISHER. There is a bunch of *aji*, then. Now who would have guessed Destiny would turn them into a candle for Kôzô. *Naruhodo!*

END OF SCENE 3.

ACT IV.

SCENE 4.

The sleeping-room in WATARU'S *house.* ADZUMA *and* WATARU *together.* ADZUMA *has been playing and singing: she lays aside the samisen, and approaches* WATARU, *who is finishing his evening repast.*

WATARU. Why that's my sun-bright wife, again! Methought to-night there hung a cloud upon the fair brow, but the pretty song hath chased it away.

ADZUMA. Have you supped well?

Myself I dressed those *aji* that you like;

Let me fill up your cup.

WAT. The wine tastes good

With such a hand to pour it. Th' *Okkasan*—

The honourable Mother—what was ill

This forenoon with her?

ADZ. Nought—save what will mend

Before to-morrow. Taste these saffron-balls

With some wild honey.

WAT. No! enough—enough!

ADZ. Ah, just one bean-cake more, or I shall think

My cooking's out of favour.

WAT. Why, you witch!

I should eat out of such deft hands as yours

Fresh come from dinner with the Emperor.

ADZ. How kind you are! In the good days gone by

Have I been what a Nippon wife should be

Wed to so dear a Lord?

WAT. My Adzuma!

Hast seen the fisher-folk, in Ise, hunt

The green sea for its wealth?   A hundred plunge,

And fetch up wrinkled shells, sea-ears, sea-fans,

Awabi, akagai.   And this man gets

Out of his fish a little pearl ; and this

Another little pearl ; and that one nought

Save slime and mud ; and that one—why, a pearl

But black and ill-shaped.   Till the one with the
>   luck,—

Not best of the band, may be — finds, in his
>   shell,

A pearl like the full moon, faultlessly white,

Round, lucent, lovely—oh ! the pride of the Sea !

Fit treasure to be button to the neck

Of our Mikado's self ; and all the crew

Envy their fellow, but no other gem

Comes like it from the secrets of the wave.

I am that fisher, sweetheart ! you that pearl.

ADZ. Oh, how I thank you !   For such pretty words

>   A cup of saké, Sir !—What happy days

Our days have been, since at the wedding-feast

We drunk nine cups together.

WAT. Have been, sweet ?

Why say you " have been " ? Please the gracious

    gods

That's but beginning ! What's to hinder us

From growing grey together, every day

Better than yesterday—till, when 'tis willed

There's to be no to-morrow, side by side,

As 'twere a-bed again, we sleep content

Under the fir-trees, in the Temple's peace ?

ADZ. Dear Lord ! if that had been—if that might be !

But some day comes the day which doth not have

Any to-morrow, and—sometimes it comes

So soon, so sudden. Did folks understand

Why Genjiro gave his life upon the wall ?

WAT. Oh, very well.

ADZ. They would not deem he died

So fond of honour that he could forget

How some must weep for him ?

WAT.   No ! I am sure

'Twas well perceived.

ADZ.   You think the living do

The dead ones justice ?   Ah ! it seems so hard

To hold in mind what wrongs the grave endures

When lips which had so much to say are closed,

And full hearts finish beating !

WAT.   Nay, my girl !

Surely a great death's like the calm that broods

At sea, after the storm.   Rude waves, ashamed,

Leave raging ;   peaks and cliffs in the true shape

Rise clear out of their shadows ;   hidden reefs

Reveal their treachery, envy's chill mist

Rolls from the prospect, and the mariner

Sees where he steered amiss.   But oh ! we talk

Like bitterns croaking.   Fill my cup again,

And fetch my robe : I have a mind to sleep.

ADZ. Yes, sleep, dear Lord !

      [*She brings in, and puts on, the night-robe of*

        WATARU ; *and then prepares his pillow, and*

> *bed-covering; while herself sitting by him,*
>
> *and taking writing materials.*]

WAT. Will you not sleep yet, wife?

ADZ. I'll write a little.

WAT. Then no *makura* !

I'll make your lap my pillow, till you come.

> [*He lies down on the sleeping-rugs, with his head*
>
> *on* ADZUMA'S *knees, and presently falls to*
>
> *slumber, while* ADZUMA *writes.*]

ADZ. He is asleep. Kind Lord! Sweet Lord! I'll talk

Soft to thy spirit through the unhearing ears.

Wataru! I am dying for thee, dear!

To-night, this night. Thou didst not, couldst

not, know

The ache of my heart, which almost cracked its

strings,

At such kind words. I dared not answer right,

For, if I answered right, I must have said

'Wataru! 'tis thy dead Adzuma speaks!'—

Husband, oh, husband! I am loath to leave

These strong true arms, this tender breast,—but,

    dear !

I *must* die ! There's no other way ! Thereby

I clear all, and I quit thee well-assured

I was thy pure wife ; body and soul thy wife,

Clean to the core in my fidelity.

How thou wilt grieve ! yet not so much, so much

As if I lived, and there fell now and then—

When people talked our story o'er again—

That one drop in Love's cup which poisons Love.

Now it can never come. When tears half dry

Thou'lt see through them that I did this thing well,

And thou wilt know there was no other way

A Nippon wife could take ; and thou wilt live

To die, I think, and have me all again,

Beyond this world. Oh, what a little while

Is left to look upon his sleeping face !

If I dared kiss it !

    [*Kissing him, a tear from* ADZUMA'S *eyes falls upon*
      WATARU'S *cheek, and awakens him.*]

WATARU (*starting up*). What, my golden girl! my

    flower!

    Weeping? I dreamed you sate in Heaven, and

    sent

    Rain down upon us.

ADZ.   Ah, forgive me, Sir:

    I have wet your beard with foolish tears. Indeed,

    You should be angry, but my heart was sad

    With one day's separation, and I mused

    How full of change life is, and how more hard

    To part for many a day.

WAT.   We will not part!

    Comfort thee, wife! and come to bed.

ADZ.   Aye, Lord!

    I'll finish these, and come. Do thou, meanwhile,

    Lie easier. [*She arranges his pillow.*]

            Sleep! But dear Wataru! Lord!

    If I should die, and thou should'st please to take

    Another happy lady in my place—

    It would be rightful—it would be thy due!—

Alas ! how then the soul of Adzuma

Would wander restless, watching whilst thou gave

Adzuma's kisses not to Adzuma.

If I did dare to ask—

WAT.   See now ; ask not !

'Tis idle torment, sweet ! this peeping-work

Into what is to be.   But I have sworn—

And I do swear again—none never shall

Lie in thy place.

ADZ.   Now gentle Heaven thank

That gracious word !   Be't the last word to-night

Dear, dearest Lord !   That kind speech on thy
   mouth

I seal with mine.   Good-night ! good-bye ! good-
   night !   [WATARU *once more falls asleep.*]
                                Now 'tis time !

He slumbers sound : my scrolls are ended : now

'Tis time ! my murderer comes, whose sword shall
   save

My name, Wataru's peace, my Mother's life,

And make them see Adzuma did not sin.

Haste, thou foiled fool, whose love was bloody
  lust,

And learn how Adzuma rights Adzuma.

First I must shear my hair away, and tie

The short ends back—Samurai-way.   [*She cuts
her hair close, and fastens the ends with a string.]

                                        So there !

My head is like Wataru's.   Next's to wet

Nape, crown, and brow.

          [*She puts water upon her head and hair.*]

                              He cannot miss to feel

This soaked hair !   Next, to leave by my Lord's
  head

The letter on his pillow.   [*She places the letter.*]

                          So ! that's done !

And here's for Mother ; she will find it there.

                        [*Places another letter.*]

Now all is wrought !   I'll to the Eastern room

And set the signal-lamp, and lie down still

In dear Wataru's place, and fold my hands,

And wait the wicked steel of Morito.

[*Exit* ADZUMA.

END OF SCENE 4.

ACT IV.

SCENE 5.

Exterior of ADZUMA'S *house. Night time. A lamp is shining through a lattice.*

Enter MORITO, *holding a naked sword.*

MORITO. Aye! there's the light! And, when I slide
    the door,

    She'll put it out, to show all's well. "All's well?"

    "All's ill"—say rather! Oh, I know, I know

    What cursed work I do, what bloody road

    I follow to the fruitage of my love ;

    And yonder light shines out of Hell, I know,

    To show my way. Well! if it gleam from Hell

It guides to Heaven, my Heaven with Adzuma.

Cut quick, fierce sword! I spit upon thy hilt

To get fast grip. Now, Lord Wataru! die!

[MORITO *enters ; and, after a brief interval, emerges*
again, carrying a head in a bloodstained cloth.]

Devils of Hell! how easy 'twas to do,

This coward murderous deed! The head was wet,

The hair cropped close. I took his girdle-purse,

That it might seem a robber's deed. Now, naught

Lives 'twixt my love and me. How sound he slept

Who doth sleep sounder now ; how soft it was

That soldier's neck! I'll to the moon-light there,

And tie my burden better.

[MORITO *goes near to a corner in the street, and*
sitting down, opens the cloth ; when there rolls
out a severed head, which is seen to be that of
ADZUMA.]

[MORITO *starts to his feet; covers his face with his*
hands, and staggers paralysed to the wall.]

MORITO [*re-approaching, after a time, the head.*]

Not his! But Adzuma's! Adzuma's head!

What ! have I murdered Adzuma ?   Hell's light !

Shrewdly thou beaconedst me !   I have steered
  straight

To damnable perdition !   Eyes ! soft eyes !

Shut, lest they blight themselves with glimpse of me,

Yes, ye are Adzuma's ; the pale cheeks her's ;

The blanched, locked lips ; her's—her's the black
  hair cropped,

And tied Wataru's way.   Oh, I see well

What snare she laid.   The savage eagle's trussed

By the white dove's small foot.   Fiends that do
  tempt,

You, Sakamune ! chief—come hither and grin !

Your utter worst is wrought !   Why then, she's
  true !

She never wrote the script !   Gods ! all reads plain

Writ in this pure bright blood.   She could not put

Our cursed plots aside, unless she died,

And so she died, making of Morito

Servant and purger to her innocence.

11

Oh, miserable Morito ! Oh, spite

Of sinfulness, mocked, to set Virtue right !

[*Exit* Morito, *carrying the head.*

END OF SCENE 5.

ACT IV.

SCENE 6.

Time, early morning. An apartment in WATARU'S *house.* KAMEJU *and a group of lamenting people discovered.* WATARU *apart, lost in grief.*

[MORITO *is seen forcing the entrance by an inner door.*]

KAMEJU. Nay, Sir ! you cannot come in. There is great woe here.

MORITO. Give me way !

KAM. Enter not, for your own comfort ! You do not know that the Lady Adzuma hath been found this morning most foully murdered.

MOR. Give me way ! Stand aside, I say ! Where is Wataru ?

KAM. He cannot speak with you.

MOR. Stand back! give way! Oh, Watanabe! Sir!

Let me have leave, and listen just so long

Till I have spoke enough to force thy blade

Make bloody period to my speech and me.

WATARU. What can'st thou say, in this fate-stricken
house,

Such heavy sorrow as to-day's could hear?

MOR. This! I am he who murdered Adzuma!

Here is her beauteous, gentle, bleeding head

Severed, in place of thine, by this vile hand!

I—fool, and beast, and butcher—being misled,

Being gone mad with passion, being beguiled,

Took her white purity for wantonness,

And forged scripts for the message of her hand.

With that, by hateful words, and cruel threats,

Perplexed her for her mother's sake, and thine,

Drove her to edge of dreadful precipice

Where no way seemed how Virtue could come safe.

Sudden resolved (—oh! as I now do know

Whispered by Heaven, which helps fidelity—)

She turns : bids me break in ; slay thee ; and then,

It should be as it should be.   Look, what's come !

How, dying, she hath shamed me.   Sir ! she lay

Meek, unafeared, in thy bed, for thy sake ;

Hair cropped, head wet, on a man's pillow put ;

And so I killed her, thinking to kill thee ;

And so I killed stone-dead the calumny

Wherewith we smirched her stainless nobleness ;

And so I killed my name, and fame, and peace,

And thy peace and the sweet joy of thy life.

And I am come, with naked breast, to lay

This fair head in thy hands, and this same sword

Which struck it off ; and to beseech of thee

Now, with its edge, to lop my head away,

Which here I bend in broken humbleness.

WAT. Thou miserable Lord, whose great sin mates

The greatness of my sorrow,—sheath the steel !

I'll use it not.   Had I encountered thee

Knowing one tittle of this before she died,

I had cloven thee, like a wolf, from chin to chine.

Hadst thou come thus, when first I found her dead,

With such a prayer,—before the half was out

I had split thy heart, if underneath such breast

Beats any heart.   But now, thy punishment

Must be to live !   Thou art crept penitent,

Ashamed, judging thyself, before my feet,

I cannot therefore kill thee.   Live ! I say

Ask no large grace like death !   Nay, see what's
    left

Upon my pillow, it shall gash thy soul

Worse than sword could thy body.

He reads ADZUMA's *last letter*.

" *To my most noble and loving Lord—Wataru
Watanabe !—I was already dead for thy peace and
honour, while we talked together this night.   When I
took boldness to ask that thou wouldest never marry
again after my death, it was my heart's deep love spoke,
rather than my duty.   I beseech you, forgive this, but
take my thanks and blessings for thy most sweet words.
Yet do thy will, and be happy.   Here, and in all the*

worlds, my heart is thine, and my soul. I have very much more to say, but tears will not suffer me to write it. Farewell! thy true and unspotted wife — in fast fidelity,   ADZUMA."

And, for her mother, this is what she left.

" I have, indeed, heard that wedded wives can be false, but I have never understood it—loving nothing so much as my husband's love, and my duty to him, and to you, mother! The nets woven around me by wicked men were very strong, and therefore I have cut them with Morito's sword. You will now know how clear I was of evil; and your life and good name will be safe, and my Lord will live in peace and honour, assured of Adzuma. I kiss the kind hand which struck me, for it was rightly done had I indeed failed so shamelessly from my fidelity. I am very sorrowful to leave you, mother, now so old and lonely; but Wataru this night — not understanding why I asked it — hath promised always to protect you. Now I die; glad because I know you will again call me your daughter Adzuma.

KAM. Oh, heart of gold! Oh! noble Nippon wife!

Oh! tender Daughter! Thou too lonely Lord,

What thinkest thou to do?

WAT. The funeral o'er

For this dear dead, I shall lay wholly down

Armour and swords, and, from this heavy time,

With shorn head, in the holy Temple's shade

A Priest I'll live, 'till good hap come to die.

MOR. I, whom thou biddest live, humbly obey,

And, with my face in the dust, take thy vow, too,

That daily, and that nightly, I may pray

For this pure soul.

WAT. Why, be it so ! And she

May thus, in Heaven, find prayers to make for

thee.

[*Exeunt Omnes.*

END OF SCENE 6.

ACT IV.

SCENE 7.

Front of a Buddhist Temple. Prayers for the dead are proceeding, and incense - sticks being burned. Buddhist monks go about the shrine; among them are seen WATARU *and* MORITO *with shaven heads, and wearing the priestly robes.* KAMEJU *stands at the foot of the Temple-steps, wearing two swords. Seeing* SAKAMUNE *pass the front of the Temple, he beckons to* MORITO, *who descends.*

KAMEJU. Master! look yonder, underneath the trees!

The Samurai!

MOR. What Samurai!

KAM.   Why he!

Damned Sakamune! Wilt thou take my sword?

    [MORITO *takes the sword and draws back his*
           priestly gown—but, with an effort, gives up
           again the weapon.]

MOR. Kameju! tempt me not. My vow is made

To spill no blood.   I were a priest forsworn

Doing this thing,—which must be done !   Go to !

[MORITO *retires into the Temple.* KAMEJU, *draw-*

ing his sword, follows SAKAMUNE, *who is*

slowly passing in the foreground.]

KAM. Ho !   Sakamune !

SAKA.   Heimin ! ha !—good-day !

KAM. No good day dawns which thou art by to blast.

Art thou come here to pray with Morito ?

SAKA. I come where I do please.

KAM.   But you go not.

Save by another road.

SAKA.   What road ?

KAM.   The road

To hell, where devils expect thee. Draw thy sword !

SAKA. I fight not with a peasant.

KAM.   Oh, for that

The hangman's knife were edge too clean for thee ;

Yet ease thy conscience.   I am Samurai,

Named yesterweek.

SAKA. (*with agitation*). I have come without my sword.

KAM. I'll lend you mine. See, here's another one !

Thy dupe, my Master, with this fateful steel

Murdered thy victim, guiltless Adzuma.

SAKA. Let me choose blades.

> [*Pretending to examine the weapons*, SAKAMUNE
> *tries to take advantage of* KAMEJU, *and to
> stab him.*]

KAM. Ah ! Villain to the last !—too base to slay

By soldier's stroke. Dog of the Samurai !

I'll rid the earth of thee. Stand, fight, and die !

> [*They fight.* SAKAMUNE *is fatally wounded, and
> falls.*]

SAKA. Curse thee, I fall ! Tell the bald-pates I die

Mocking at simpletons.　　　[SAKAMUNE *dies.*]

KAM. [*slowly wiping his blade, and looking down upon
the dead man.*]

　　　　　　　　　Good sword ! forgive

I stained thee so ! But, see, he could not live !

THE END.

www.ingramcontent.com/pod-product-compliance
Lightning Source LLC
Chambersburg PA
CBHW022359020726

47500CB00002B/358